Dope Girl 2
Daddy's Little Girl

Sa'id Salaam

Prologue

"You're a hunter, a lion, a tiger, a predator. You have to eat to live, and you must kill to eat. You don't eat; you die. Now what you gonna do, eat or starve? Live or die?"

"I'ma eat, Granddaddy. I'ma kill," Cameisha replied to her grandfather's posthumous coaching as she stalked her prey.

She was just like a lion, indeed, as she crept forward unseen. Instead of tall grass to conceal her approach, she blended into the ghetto landscape. Her disguise was perfect for this urban jungle. She fit right in.

Tovia looked back at the bag lady with contempt. It seemed the same dirty hobo had been following her for the last few nights. She had been but never this close. She hoped the old hag would beg her for some spare change. She squeezed the knife in her pocket in anticipation. All she had coming was some spare stitches. Ironically, it was the exact same knife that got her into this trouble.

Cutting through the darkened park in the Bronx at night wasn't the best idea but since it shaved a few blocks off her trip, she made the gamble. After dunking chicken in hot grease, anything that could get her in a hot shower was an option. When she noticed the bag lady had gotten too close for comfort, she stopped to confront her.

"Fuck you following me or something!" Tovia spun and demanded. A press of a button flicked the shiny switch blade open.

"Shole is," the bag lady replied in a deep southern drawl. The bright clean smile was incongruous to the filthy clothes and hair. She pulled the wig off to answer the 'where do I know you' question contorting her prey's face.

"You!" Tovia announced, seeing Cameisha clearly. She dropped her knock-off purse and prepared for battle. "You must miss your buddy Angie, huh? Don't worry, you bout to see her real quick."

"One of us is, that's for sho," Meisha replied, getting into a defensive stance.

2

Cameisha had a gun—a cute little 40 cal but didn't pull it. She was going Old Testament tonight: An eye for an eye, a tooth for a tooth. That meant Tovia was getting stabbed.

The combatants circled, looking for the chance to strike. Meisha gave her a false opening, and she eagerly took it.

Tovia thrust the dagger at her torso, giving Meisha a chance to apply some of Karate Joe's teaching. A beautiful counter move was executed to perfection as she side-stepped the lunge and grabbed her wrist and arm. Once the wrist was bent past the point that wrists were designed to be bent, the knife came free. Cameisha grabbed it and rammed it into Tovia's face. Her first thought was to run until the unexpected happened.

"Huh?" Tovia asked curiously as Meisha handed the knife back. She wisely accepted it then foolishly made the same move with the same results.

Only this time, Cameisha stabbed her in her arm before giving the knife back. She gave it back, and the cycle repeated itself. It was like something out of a Jackie Chan movie. Over and over, she got stabbed in different parts of her body. The wounds weren't fatal; they were torture. It was only when one of the blows nicked her femoral artery that Cameisha decided to cut short her fun. Without medical attention, the girl would be dead in minutes, only she didn't have minutes left. Her book of life was flipped to its final page as Meisha tried to return the knife one last time.

"Nuh uh!" Tovia said, shaking her head vigorously at the outstretched knife. "You keep it!"

That brought a quick smile to Cameisha's face, but it quickly morphed into a mask of murder. Play time was over; it was time to die. She rushed forward and drove the long slender blade into Tovia's forehead. It was buried in her brain up to the hilt.

Tovia looked confused as her eyes fluttered, trying to bring death into focus. She looked like she wanted to say something but couldn't find the words. Maybe she would figure it out in the afterlife because this one was over.

"Go on and die now. I gotta go home and get packed. I'm going to college!" Cameisha urged proudly.

Tovia frowned but complied and dropped dead. Gloves ensured the knife in her head didn't bare any fingerprints on them. She shed her dirty disguise and dumped it in the park's dumpster as she made her exit. It was a clean murder just like she had been taught. No witnesses, no DNA, no nothing. She was just like daddy.

Chapter 1

"Bitch, you sound crazy! Yo' ass is twenty-two talking about some damn college! Fuck outta here, bitch, this aint no *It's a Different World*," Keisha chided.

Jackie's cousin wasn't shit and wanted some company in her miserable existence. She was born and raised in the projects and intended to die there. This was her life, and she was cool with it.

"You need to bring your ass down to the club tonight. First, we gotta get yo' ass some clothes. Fuck you got on? The prison don't give y'all nothing when they let you out? You look a mess. Anyway, I'ma clean you up, meet the right baller, and come up."

Jackie only half-listened to the negligible advice until, finally, she just saw her mouth moving a hundred miles an hour. The words had blended into the medley of sounds that was Harlem. Mookie was yelling at Jo-Jo; Quinta was laughing with La-La; car horns were honking; sirens were blaring; and—as usual—some one was shooting.

On one hand, yeah, she would be the oldest incoming freshman, but it beat the title she currently held as the oldest chick in the projects without a kid. God is indeed most gracious and most merciful and spared her from having a child with her infamous ex-boyfriend.

Sure, the nickname 'Lil Ill Will' would have been ill, but since she put a bullet in daddy's forehead, it would make growing up a little uncomfortable. Finding out your parents were Jack and Ill could either work for or against you.

"Bitch, last week I met this nigga name . . . uh . . . named? Anyway, I met this nigga last week who gave me a hundred bucks just to hang out in the V.I.P. with him. I ain't have to fuck him or nothing. Just gave him a little head under the table and . . ."

After ten years of the free world prison that was life with Ill Will and another two in real prison, Jackie wanted nothing more than to put this past life behind. She wanted out of Harlem with a passion.

Her mother retired from her career as a crackhead by dying of AIDS the same day Jackie got out. She made it to the hospice just in time to hear her mother's last words before her last breath.

"Leave," she pleaded, looking up at the pretty black girl staring down at her. "Baby, get out them projects and never come back."

"Okay, Ma," Jackie said just before the angel of death came to take what he was sent for.

While in prison, Jackie applied for and was granted a full scholarship. It included all tuition, room and board, meals, and a twenty-five dollar weekly stipend for etceteras. You can't really buy a lot of etceteras for twenty-five bucks, but it beats a blank.

She would be traveling light because she didn't have shit—a few dated outfits from the Goodwill, the cheap sweater the prison gave her, and very little self-esteem. Half of the small check they gave her went for mismatched three-pack panties, bras, and toiletries.

"I fuck Petey once a week for weed. When Big Lou come pick up Lil Lou, I suck a few bucks out of him. Nigga don't wanna fuck 'cause he married. So what, I'm his baby mama!" Keisha ranted. "Oh, and Sherrod keep a bitch hair done for some head. Head for head, fair exchange ain't robbery. I fucked . . ."

Jackie was broken down like a horse with no name. She was as docile as a church mouse despite being the killer that she was. Otha had dumped her once he found out how close he had come to becoming her fourth kill. The police called it self-defense since Will was in his apartment with a gun but still prosecuted Jackie for the dirty gun. The only thing that gave her solace was the look of shock on Ill Will's face when she shot him.

The last two weeks she'd spent with her cousin since being released from prison were worse than prison itself. Actually, prison was pretty easy since she became an unwilling lesbian—letting a stud feed, protect, and suck orgasms out of her. Beat the hell out of getting the hell beat out of you like what happened to a lot of girls. In prison, girls without a gang, clique, or stud were preyed upon.

The bad black girl caused quite a stir among the studs as she and the other new arrivals arrived. Jolline, being the alpha male, was given first crack at her. Either that or get fucked up.

"A-yo, ma, check it," Jolline spat as only one from Brooklyn can. "It's rough in here. You can do an easy bid with me or a hard one with them."

As Jackie processed the words, along with their implications, she watched one of the girls who rode the bus with her being robbed. One gang of girls swatched all her property followed by two more who took her sneakers. Right after that, three girls dragged her kicking and screaming into a cell to be raped. They took the only thing she had left.

"You can get with that, or you can get with this," Jolline offered and lolled out her long lizard like tongue and rubbed her chin hairs with it.

The combination of fear and slight curiosity led her to accept the offer. That night, Jolline loaded her locker box with all the extras that helped prison become almost bearable. She then treated her to the first oral sex of her life. It helped the time pass but only pushed her further into submission

"Bitch, you sound crazy! And even if yo' ass do go to college, you still ain't gone be better than no one. I coulda went to college too," Keisha yelled to her cousin's departing back.

She berated her all the way down the hall. Jackie dipped into the staircase to escape the torment, walking down the pissy stairs beat getting insulted. However, Keisha was waiting on her. She hung her head out the window and hurled more insults at her as she walked quickly through the courtyard. Once she was out of sight, Keisha fell back on the sofa and cried. Poor thing didn't have anyone to be miserable with.

Jackie boarded the bus to the train to the plane without a side-eyed glance at the city she was leaving behind. It was good riddance as far as she was concerned. Ironically, her worldly possessions fit in a bag just small enough for the overhead storage. Once the plane was airborne, she cast a woeful glance at New York City like it would be her last. It wouldn't be, but it would be her last time not having shit.

Chapter 2

"Child, you are going to miss your flight playing around," Deidra yelled to Cameisha in the back of the apartment.

"I'ma freat it like this!" Dasia insisted, showing off a new move she planned to introduce to the now ubiquitous fat-fat dance.

"I'm coming!" Meisha yelled over the music and through the door. The festive mood turned somber in an instant. The urge to go was stronger than the one to stay, so she resumed packing.

Having way too much stuff gave her a chance to give a lot of stuff away. A lot of stuff she bought to give away anyway. That's why some of it was in Aqua's size.

"Aqua, I need your . . . umm . . . special talent," Cameisha asked.

"Oh, is that what you call it?" Aqua quipped as she sat on the stuffed suitcase so it could be zipped up.

Dasia's face crinkled at the finality of the bag being closed. Her bottom lip quivered in a futile attempt not to cry.

"Girl, what's wrong with you?" Meisha asked when she saw her friend's state.

"Nothing," Dasia lied, despite the tears falling freely from her eyes.

"Aww, come here, chica," Cameisha said with outstretched arms.

Dasia took her up on the offer and rushed in to the embrace. Aqua came over and wrapped them both in her meaty arms. Together, they sniffled and moaned like they just lost the championship, which would be cool for girls, but six-feet, ten-inch men crying over a game is creepy. Man the fuck up.

"Look, guys, I left y'all ten pounds of weed. The spot booming, and Sincerity gone mess with y'all on the re-up. Y'all good?"

"Yeah, we cool." Dasia sniffled, trying to regain her usual cool. She pulled away and swatted the tears from her now puffy face. "We got this. Go do you."

"Dasia!" Cameisha called after her as she stormed off.

"She just gone miss you," Aqua explained their friend's sudden departure. "Me too."

"I'ma miss y'all too. See, if y'all would have graduated, y'all would be coming with me," she reminded.

"Next year!" Aqua cheered, actually believing it herself.

"Next year," Cameisha repeated as if she believed it too.

"Girl, if we don't leave this apartment this instant, you are going to miss your flight! You can just stay here," Deidra demanded, sticking her head in.

That did the trick and put some pep in her step. Cameisha had seen enough of the Bronx. In the couple of years she had lived here, she witnessed more death and destruction than she thought possible. She wanted nothing more than to put the thousand miles distance from here to school between her. She and Aqua shared a fake smile to mask the pain of departure, but it didn't last.

"I'ma miss you." Aqua waited and snatched her back into her arms.

"Me . . . argh . . . too," Cameisha managed from the vice like grip.

They rocked and sobbed, sobbed and rocked, until grandma broke it up. Aqua grabbed a large suitcase in each hand while Meisha slung the tote over her back.

The project dwellers watched the exodus with mixed emotions. A medley of regret, pride, and envy was felt from the various sets of eyes that followed them out. Some prayed she would make it big and never return. Others prayed she would fail and keep their misery company. One wanted to beg to come with her. Most were stuck because project life only prepares you for project life.

The car service had sent an SUV to make the trip out to JFK airport. Cameisha studied the city with the finality of someone not planning to return. She was getting one for the road, implanting one last visual. Ask anyone who escaped from New York and they'd explain what it was like.

Grandma's threats of missing the first flight were highly embell-ished. In today's culture, a person has to arrive damn near a day in ad-vance just to get through the security procedures. Those procedures forced Grandmother and Grandchild to say their goodbyes at the tick-et counter. The best friends waved and blew kisses until they were out of sight.

A short plane ride and even shorter cab trip later, Cameisha was in front of her dorm at Atlanta College. She was on her own at that point and struggled to get her luggage to the curb. Since this was the all-girls dorm, there wasn't a dude in sight. Not this early in the day, but come sundown, thirsty niggas would flock here like it was a desert oasis. In a way it was, only here you could wet your dick instead of your whistle. The building was rapidly filling with teenage girls and a couple of not so girls.

"You need some help with your bag, sweetness," a baritone voice asked from behind.

Meisha immediately switched into damsel in distress mode. She turned with fluttering eyelashes and a smile that quickly turned into a scowl.

"I'm cool yo!" she spat viciously at the flirting stud smiling down at her. She had switched into battle mode, proving you can take a chick out of the South Bronx, but you can't take the South Bronx out of a chick. Even if that chic is imported.

"Aight, shawty. If'n you need anything," the stud paused to lick her lips to demonstrate how she licked lips, "holla at Scrappy."

Cameisha was 38 hot at the come on and lugging those heavy ass bags up to the third floor turned up the heat. She found her room and burst in ready to fall over from exhaustion. The shell shocked inhabi-tant jumped up ready to flee like a frightened deer.

"Fuck wrong with you?" Meisha barked at the sudden move then caught herself. "I mean hey. I'm Cameisha, your new roommate.

"Um, I um, I'm Jackie," Jackie stammered and lowered her head into submission.

When they shook hands, it was the innocolous beginning of a deadly alliance. She looked a lot younger than her twenty-two years, and her meekness brought a frown to Cameisha's face.

"Where you from?" Cameisha wondered aloud.

"Harlem," Jackie told her. She looked down at her cheap sneakers and then at her new friends expensive pair. "How bout you?"

"The Bronx yo," she replied proudly as if she really was.

After the introductions were made, they both turned to unpack. Three minutes later, Jackie was finished and sat down. Cameisha struggled to fit too much stuff into not enough space.

"You can use some of my drawers 'cause my stuff . . uhh . . ." Jackie offered, struggling with an excuse for not having shit.

"Okay, thanks!" Cameisha cheered.

She liked the timid girl at that moment, but it wouldn't last long.

Chapter 3

Atlanta College was, in a word, turned the fuck up. Just like most colleges across the country, it was packed to the gills with oversexed teens on their own for the first time in their short lives. Once music, drugs, and alcohol were stirred into the mix, most would lose their damn minds.

A good fourth of incoming freshman would not become sophomores—for a variety of reasons. Since more than mere attendance was required to pass, the slackers would fail. Quite a few would end up pregnant and drop out to go struggle. Some were going to die. It was inevitable that some would get murdered, and there would be a suicide or two. Not to mention, drug overdoses and alcohol poisonings. Some dumb ass rapper made it cool to sip cough syrup, and kids were putting themselves to sleep forever like unwanted dogs at the pound. They came with book bags and went home in body bags.

Some were going to party like rock stars even though they were not. The sheltered kids usually fell off first. Going from zero to sixty would prove to be too much for quite a few. Non-stop partying took its toll on them. First, grades slip, attendance wanes, classes get dropped, and next thing you know it's, "Welcome to Burger Shack, can I take your order?" Why do you think the cashiers have attitudes? Because they fucked up at school and had to come home in disgrace.

Others would have that first drink and like it. That would lead to their first joint, and they would like that too. Once they were high, why not pop a pill and get a little higher? Makes sense, doesn't it? Next thing you know, a Chronicles of a Junky book is being written about them. The co-ed . . . hmm?

Atlanta College featured several housing options, but once Grandma got wind of the female-only dorm, she called in a favor to get Cameisha in. It was long-distance cock blocking. Jackie was selected at random and assigned the room in the dick-free dorm.

"Ooh, they got Shepherd's Pie!" Jackie announced triumphantly as she read the menu.

"My favorite!" Cameisha lied. In truth, she could afford to eat out and avoid the bland institutional food served in the school's cafeteria, but she wanted the complete college experience.

"Want some more?" Cameisha asked as Jackie scraped her plate empty. The few bites she ate satisfied the college experience, and she was going to order a pizza.

"Mmhm." Jackie grinned and snatched the plate away. Her buddy watched as she quickly scarfed it down.

As they walked back over to the dorm, they spied a lock party being set up on one of the outdoor baskeball courts. This would be the first party of the school year and a must for the freshman.

"Yo, we gotta get fly and hit that!" Meisha gushed.

"You go head. I gotta . . . um, study." Jackie lied.

"Study what? We ain't even been to class yet."

"I know, but I gotta . . ."

"Say no more. I got you," Meisha said, understanding her dilemma. The girl barely had a stitch of clothes.

Since Jackie was taller and thicker than Cameisha, borrowing a pair of jeans was out of the question. They settled on a summer dress that looked so much better on its guest than its owner. Cameisha decided she didn't want it back. The bright yellow dress contrasted the black skin so well it would make bumblebees jealous.

Not to be outdone, Meisha squeezed into a pair of snug jeans that made her ass look like she was trying to smuggle a basketball into the party. The tight tee showed off her nice chest as it advertised its design-er. Crispy white sneakers set off the casual ensemble.

The first thing that hit the girls when they stepped onto the court was the smell. Damn near everyone was smoking weed. Every group, couple, or solo person was passing or puffin' on a blunt. The dope girl couldn't help but multiply each blunt by the bucks. Somebody just made an easy grand she surmised.

"The thing about hustling, you never really stop."

"Nuh uh, Daddy!" Meisha whined as the memory came to mind.

"Huh?" Jackie asked, thinking she was talking to her.

"Uh, nothing. Ooh, that's my shit!" Cameisha exclaimed as Erv-G's latest jam pounded through the speakers. She rushed to the makeshift dance floor to show them how the Fat-Fat dance was really done.

Jackie suddenly felt ancient as she watched the kids' party. It broke her hear that her whole life was spent in one jail or another. First was the prison of the projects. Sure, you could come and go, but no one was really free. Generations had served life sentences in the red brick prison. Her crackhead mother and deadbeat boyfriend were her jailers. Their mental, verbal, and physical abuse had reduced her to a zombie. A deer scared of its shadow, ready to flee. Zero self-esteem made her easy prey.

"Sup cutie?" a cute teen asked, offereing a smile along with the question. Jackie frowned, and then leaned back assuming whoever this 'cutie' he was talking to was behind her. "I'm talking to you."

"Me?" Jackie asked, looking confused. She even pointed at herself for clarification.

"Yeah you! Don't tell me you ain't know you was a cutie." He laughed. "I'm Marquis."

She stifled a giggle with her hand. "Jackie."

"So, Jackie, you want a beer?"

"Yes," she replied, even though she didn't drink.

"Wanna smoke a blunt?"

"Yes," came the reply, even though she didn't smoke. Jackie was so tickled by the attention she answered yes to his every question.

"Wanna go to your room? Can I have a kiss? Can I hit it?"

"Yes, yes, yes, yes."

"The fuck?" was the question on Cameisha's mind when she returned to where she left her purse with her friend and found neither. She scanned the packed area with a scowl until she came across a brilliant smile.

Curt was a six-foot, four-inch point guard on the school's team. He was as handsome as he was good and had the groupies to prove it. He was surrounded by several pretty girls all yapping at him at once. The politicians smile pasted on his face was meant to placate them. It was obvious he wasn't paying them any attention. How could he when Cameisha had his full attention.

The smile became real, but it still wasn't returned. Cameisha was far too concerned with the contents of her purse. Yeah, he was cute, but where was her phone? Still, she didn't take her eyes off of him. They engaged in a full court staring contest until Meisha won by default.

The appearance of a beautiful girl came and stole the show. The groupies all got ghost when the light-skinned, brown-haired, curvy, little thing showed up. She tip-toed up and planted a kiss on Curt's lips. Arnell followed his gaze over to Cameisha. She scrunched up her face as she studied Cameisha. Declaring her as no threat, she turned her attention back to her boyfriend. They were the school's version of a celebrity couple. The typical sports star dates head cheerleader scenario.

Meisha now had someone else to amuse her as she studied the girl. Arnell was gorgeous but full of drama and extremely animated. She made a variety of facial expressions as she rambled on to her boyfriend. Not just the run of the mill smiles and frowns. She had some complex combinations to express her inner thoughts. She might lift one brow, curl her lip, and cock her head to one side to express herself or an even more complex series of eye flutters combined with a half-smile, half-frown, and giggle.

Meisha watched with amusement as Curt stared back lustfully. The pretty new girl would make a nice addition to his 'I hit that list'. Every man had one—yes, even *your* man. Go ask him. It's not to be confused with a 'hit list', which is active. The 'I hit that' list comes in handy when out with the fellas and a pretty girl happens by; you can say, "I hit that."

She got tired of watching the Arnell Show at the same time she gave up on looking for her friend. It wasn't like she didn't know where Jackie lived, so that's where she went.

Cameisha declined all offers as she weaved her way through the crowd of weaved girls and wannabe thugged out college boys. Too bad black boys want to dress like goons when they aren't. She marched back to the dorm like a North Korean solider in anger. As she did, she noticed—and wondered—why the school was dead in the middle of the hood. It was surrounded by projects on two sides, but they somehow didn't show up in the brochure pictures.

"Leave the projects a thousand miles away and still in the damn projects."

She was already feeling some kinda way but finding the room door ajar only added to it. It was bad enough her purse was gone, but all the rest of her stuff was inside. It went from bad to worse when she saw Jackie and Marquis having sex.

"Say, shawty, give us a second . . . or you can stay," Marquis announced at the intrusion. He was about to dismiss her, until he saw how pretty she was. Now he put on his best stroke to impress her as Jackie covered her face with her pillow.

"Nigga, your second was up the second you came in my damn room!" Meisha spat. She was about to really go in, but dude grunted and contorted, signaling that his second was indeed up.

She frowned in disgust and turned her wrath on her bunkmate still hiding behind her pillow. "How the fuck you got some nigga up in here?"

"You gotta go," Jackie meekly told her guest.

Marquis was done anyway and pulled his bare dick out and stood to get dressed. He put a little sway in his hips when he saw Meisha staring at his wood. It was far from a lustful gaze as she shook her head in dismay. The man she loved burned her from unprotected sex; what would a stranger give you?

Jackie snatched the sheet over herself and stared up at the ceiling. She was confused at why her friend was so upset, and now her boyfriend left without leaving a number or saying goodbye.

"Umm . . . earth to Jackie. Hello!!" Cameisha demanded, coming closer and yelling louder.

"Yes," she answered softly, afraid to look up at her.

"Look, I don't give a fuck about you fucking some nigga you met two seconds ago, but I do care about you doing it up in here! And how the fuck you gone run off with my shit and leave me at the party?"

"I'm sorry."

"Sorry? That's your answer to all them questions, you sorry! You sorry alright, sorry excuse for a woman. You sure you from Harlem 'cause . . . "

Jackie tuned out the yelling as she had done her whole life. It was just like with Ill Will, just like with her mother. She was never good enough, always in trouble. Cameisha's mouth moved rapidly, but Jackie didn't hear one word. She wished she or her could just disappear.

"We gotta stay up in this bitch, fine, but I don't fuck with you. Don't fuckin' talk to me. Don't touch my shit. Don't . . . "

Chapter 4

Meanwhile, back in the Bronx, Dasia and Aqua were attempting to break the world record for shortest time to fuck a package up. Ironically, the record was held by Jackie's late boyfriend Ill Will. He got popped trying to sell nine ounces to an undercover shortly after buying it.

The girls had two major obstacles in their path to flip the ten pounds of weed. The first was their own weed habits. They were both potheads. It took an early morning blunt to get them started then followed up at regular intervals to maintain their high. Staying high and being productive do not go hand-in-hand. They don't even know each other.

Marijuana contains the compound THC, which causes the euphoric high weed heads love so much. It's what makes you happy when you smoke. It also contains a liberal dose of 'fuck it'. Fuck it is the chemical substance that affects the part of the brain that controls motivation. A person would still be able to acknowledge all the things they must, should, and supposed to do, and then just say, "fuck it." It can make you lazy in small amounts but too much leads to a grinding halt in productivity.

Instead of hitting the block to hustle, the girls spent most of the day watching videos or movies while smoking and eating. Dudes would have to knock on their door to buy a bag of Fat-Fat. If and when they got up to serve them, then came their second problem.

Both girls were addicted to dick. The plain yet pretty Dasia could do a lot better than being a jump off, but low self-esteem convinced her otherwise. She was so excited to get attention, especially by the cute guys with diva girlfriends, she was bait. And Aqua was, of course, Aqua. Her esteem was plenty high. You couldn't tell big girl she wasn't fly. It was her low IQ that gave her problems. Lack of education leads to becoming a slave to desires. If it felt good, she was with it.

Once word got out about the dunces with the good weed, guys flocked to them. They would gladly hang out with them for free weed and pussy. Soon, they were crediting and borrowing weed that would never be paid for.

E-Baby controlled the drug trade two blocks over on 164th. He was a grown ass man but had no qualms about beating the girls out of their package. Back when Meisha had it pumping, he felt a pinch in his pocket. He started to send a squad of youngins over to the project to rob them, until he heard she was related to Killa. E-Baby was old enough to know what that meant.

He settled on just conning the girls out of their weed. Aqua would have been easier, but Dasia was cute. He decided to trade the pretty brown thing some dick for dope. It took a day of staking out the bodega for him to catch his prey. She actually planned on working that day and had on her Fat-Fat short set. Cameisha, the marketing specialist that she was, had short sets made with their product name Fat-Fat on the chest and ass. Worked like a charm.

"Sup beautiful?" E-Baby asked, standing over Dasia at the counter. He was close enough for her to smell his Sandlewood oil, and she was drunk off it.

"Fine," Dasia sang, ready to fall into his arms.

That's exactly what she did. The next time she looked up he was on top and inside of her. The grown man put it on the teen so good the rest was easy.

"How much of that weed you got left?" E-Baby asked a second after she had the first orgasm of her life.

"Fine," she sang again, as if it answered the question. "Oh . . . uh . . . about five pounds."

"Tell you what, since you and me go tougher now, bring it all to me, and I'ma knock it off for you."

"You for real?" Dasia exclaimed at both offers. "I am? You will?"

"Sure! You my girl, ma. Bring me the weed. I'll sell it and call you when it's done so you can get your money."

I guess I don't have to tell you that call never came. Dasia waited patiently—then not so patiently—for weeks and nothing. Finally, she worked up the nerve to walk over and confront him. Aqua came with her for moral support and because she was sober, broke, and hungry. They found E-Baby sitting on the stairs to his building like a king on his throne.

"Uh uh! Who deze bitches?" Meka squealed from her seat between his legs. Her crew of hood rats all came closer for inspection.

"Um, can I talk to you?" Dasia asked timidly.

"No," E-Baby replied casually then went back to watching his workers work the block.

"I need my money," she whined desperately, but it fell on deaf ears. He didn't even look in her direction.

"I need my money," Meka mocked, cracking her cronies up.

"Y'all bitches need to stop," one of the ratchet girls demanded too close to Aqua's ear and got knocked out for it.

Meka was next to get knocked out when she leapt from her porch and was met by one of Aqua's meaty mitts. The rest of the girls jumped in but got nowhere. The young boys on the block had to intervene to beat them up properly. Dasia and Aqua limped back to the projects bloodied, battered, and bruised. Not knowing what else to do, they returned to their reserved bench in the courtyard and moped. That's exactly where Sincerity found them.

"The fuck wrong with y'all?" she asked, stifling a laugh. She could only shake her head as she listened to their story. She was moved, but not moved enough to do anything. They were, after all, not her problem. She did make a call on their behalf once she got upstairs.

"Sup, chica, let me tell you bout yo' girls," she cackled when Meisha picked up in Atlanta.

Chapter 5

College English was a required course, but Cameisha looked forward to it with zeal. She always had a passion for reading and recently decided she wanted to be an author. Why not, everyone else was. That, of course, was in addition to being a doctor, a lawyer, a vet, and a model. And an astronaut . . . and dentist . . . and social worker . . . and . . .

The professor was a dreamy African-American man in his early forties. A slight streak of grey decorated his temples, framing a chiseled chestnut face. He spoke in measured tones with the bass in his voice turned to high. Women often got caught up in the sounds eminating from his thick lips instead of the words they carried, young girls as well.

Cameisha let out a schoolgirl sigh as she listened to him introduce himself and his class. Mr. Woods, as he called himself, had her full attention. She only half-noticed the fashionably late students slink in and scramble for the remaining empty seats. She did notice Curt when he made his next appearance into her life. She tried not to stare as he surveyed the room but got caught up in his cool. When their eyes locked, he decided the empty seat next to her was his.

Curt led a trail of batting eyes as he made his way over to where Cameisha sat. He sat down, leaned back, and waited. The popular point guard was so used to girls throwing themselves at him, he expected the pretty girl to do so too. Good thing he wasn't holding his breath because she was too busy soaking up her first class to be concerned with him.

"Hey, I'm . . . "

"Shhh!" Meisha demanded, killing the introduction that threatened to make her miss one of Mr. Woods's words.

He frowned from being shushed for the first time in his life. He had no comeback for being rejected, and it confused him. It wasn't his first time being confused in the class. Actually, since he kept failing it, it was his third time being confused.

"Get up. I need to sit next to him," a dangerously close voice demanded getting her attention.

Cameisha prayed a silent prayer that whoever it was was not talking to her. She glared up to see Arnell standing over her, tapping her foot impatiently, waiting for her command to be carried out. Getting into another first day of school fist fight would not go well with Grandma. Especially since this was college, but it looked to be inevitable. Still, she was polite.

"Can you please back the fuck up?" Meisha asked, offering a fake smile.

"Excuse me?" Arnell frowned, raised a brow, and wiggled her nose. That was her perplexed face.

"If you want to sit next to him, then both of y'all go find a seat together!" she growled through clenched teeth.

Curt watched proudly at another episode of drama started behind him. The exchange caught the attention of those closest who turned to look, which in turn caused the rest of the class to turn to look, which caught the attention of the star of the show.

"Ladies, would you care to join us?" the professor professed with a bright smile that masked his ire.

"Yes, I would. Can you please ask this, this . . . "Arnell studied Cameisha's ponytail, sweats, and sneakers before deciding on, "ragamuffin to move out of my seat."

"Come on, Arnell. We'll move to another spot," Curt said, rising from his chair, putting the bulge in his pants eye level with Cameisha.

Cameisha was mad at herself for letting her gaze linger longer than it should have on his crotch. It awakened the part of a woman that likes that part of a man. She was even madder at being called a ragamuffin and thought about beating her up. Curt led his demented diva away so class could resume.

She had a ball in the class watching the animated instructor instruct. Likewise, her next class was a blast as well. But as soon as it was over, the memory of the insult came rushing back to mind.

"What the hell is a ragamuffin anyway?" she wondered aloud as she walked back to the dorm.

Already fuming when she got to her room, it only got worse when she walked in. There was her roommate in a downward facing dog yoga position getting vigorous back shots from a dude. A dude obviously late for something the way he was hitting it a hundred miles an hour.

"Out, out!" Cameisha shouted and pulled the student out of her roommate by his shoulder.

"Fuck wrong with you, bitch!" he demanded, getting a busted lip for using the magic word.

"I got yo' bitch, bitch," she shouted, putting her dukes up for battle.

He jumped up with his bare dick bobbing in the air. The cute suburban boy had never had a fight in his life and decided now was not the time to start. Not with that look in the girl's eye.

"Y'all crazy!" He settled for and quickly dressed as Jackie pulled her cover over her nakedness.

"Call me," Jackie moaned as he rushed out.

Nevermind, she didn't have a number to even give him.

"Now you!" Meisha shouted, turning her attention to her roommate. "Get up. I need a one!"

"I don't wanna fight you," Jackie pleaded.

"You must, 'cause you keep violating our space! We been here a damn week, and you fucked three different dudes already! Fuck you selling pussy or some shit?"

"He said I was pretty," Jackie whispered solemnly. It sounded crazy to her, too, when she heard it aloud, but it was true.

Gary sat next to her in algebra and told her she was pretty. He saw the giggle and blush in her black skin and moved in for the kill. He flattered his way into an afternoon roll in the hay.

"And? You fucked him 'cause he told you that? Shit, you are pretty."

"You really think I'm pretty?" she gushed, jumping up from the bed to hear the answer better.

"Uh, yeah, but I don't wanna fuck you." Meisha frowned. "Yo, you need to get yourself together."

"I'm trying," Jackie said sadly as she sat back down.

Tears began to stream from her eyes. It took a full ten minutes before she could regain her composure. Cameisha couldn't help but to feel sorry for her.

"Yo, you from New York; you ever heard of Jack and Ill?"

"The stick up kids? Of course," Meisha asked, wondering where she was going with this.

"Well, I'm Jack," she confessed and commenced to confess the whole story—the abuse, the robberies, the murders. Laid out all the sordid details, and Cameisha didn't believe a word of it.

"Get the fuck outta here!" She laughed then cracked the fuck up. She was laughing as hard as Jackie had been crying a few minutes ago. She now had tears running down her face as well. "Girl, you scared of your own damn shadow, and you expect me to believe you a killer? I'm more of a killer than you!"

Cameisha heard her own last words as soon as they left her mouth. She *was* a killer. She killed Big Bessie and Old Man Grimes back home and just recently murdered Tovia. She would have killed the dealers from Nelson Avenue had she not traded being a dope girl for a college girl. Instead of regret, she felt nothing.

"Anyway, let's make a deal," Meisha offered.

"What kinda deal?" Jackie asked eagerly. She was so happy her roommate wasn't mad at her anymore she would have agreed to almost anything. Scratch that, she would have agreed to anything. She jumped up again, bouncing with excitement.

"Okay, first, I'ma need you to put some clothes on 'cause . . . umm, yeah."

"My bad." Jackie giggled and complied.

"A'ight you, look. You pretty; you fine, so you ain't gotta keep fucking to prove it. We a team now. You hold me down; I hold you down. I eat; you eat," Cameisha proclaimed.

"That's a bet!" Jackied accepted and rushed over to seal the deal with a hug.

A deadly merger was formed just like that.

Chapter 6

When the weekend rolled around the new BFFs decided to hit a party. First, they had to decide which party to hit because there were so many to choose from. It seemed every frat, sorority, group, or clique was throwing one.

The light-skinned sorority was having an all light party. They had a paper bag at the door to see who could be admitted inside. A recent driver's license or I.D. could vouch for you if you had a tan. The only thing dark in the house was the humor.

The faux gangters and wanna be hoochie mamas were throwing a bash. The sheltered poacher kids and nerds dressed in sagging jeans and short skirts to emulate the bad boys and girls they admired. The same ones they left home to go to school while they went to morgues, prisons, and abortion clinics. Funny thing is . . . bad kids never pretend to be good kids.

Then there was the Phi Alpha something frat. This was the one all the athletes and elite guys beloned to. This was the one Curt belonged to. The cost of admission was a dime. Meaning you had to be one to get in. Bad bitches only, and Meisha and Jackie all dressed up were two bad bitches.

"Okay, I'm getting tired of my clothes looking better on you than me," Meisha quipped lightheartedly yet half-serious.

Everytime she let her thicker roommate borrow a garment, she filled it out to perfection. Pride often led her to donate it to Jackie's cause. Slowly, her empty closet began to fill.

"I look okay?" Jackie pleaded desperately, needing approval. Since she stopped sleeping with every dude who looked at her, she turned exclusively to Cameisha to boost her self-esteem. She, like a lot of girls, hadn't figured out the self part of self-esteem—do it your damn self.

She turned sideways to inspect herself in the full length mirror, but it couldn't hold all that ass poking out the back. They recently discovered that Cameisha's loose-fitting, casual jeans fit her like a glove. Add a designer Tee and viola! Instant bad bitch.

"You aight," Meisha teased as she squeezed into a pair of tight jeans herself.

She still wan't completely comfortable with all the attention her round ass drew, but Curt would be there. Curt being there meant Arnell would be there, and she wanted to look good for the both of them.

Jackie left her long, black hair all the way down, giving her an exotic East Indian look. Cameisha let her natural curls frame her pretty face. They each sprayed themselves from Cameisha's growing perfume collection and stepped into their sandals.

Cheerfully, they stepped out into the hall and were met by a bunch of long faces. Girls roamed the hall on the verge of tears with pained expression on their faces.

"What's wrong? Someone die? Facebook crashed?" Meisha asked their neighbor Cynthia.

"No, worse!" she cried out with her lip quivering from the sorrow. "No one has any weed. I called everyone. You don't have any do you?"

"Uh . . . no," Cameisha said, fighting not to laugh for the umpteenth time. She wished she did.

She peeped that a student with a solid connect of even mediocre weed could really come up. Music videos made drug use cool, and since everyone wanted to be cool, everyone smoked weed. Some did pills, most drank, but damn near everyone smoked.

The current campus weed man was a herb from Middle America somewhere. Turbo, as he called himself, did okay in high school selling weed to his classmates. He came to college with a pound of mid-grade grown by his older brother. It sold out quickly, and he had been struggling to maintain a supply ever since.

The surrounding ghetto had plenty of drugs, but the local thugs preyed on the college kids. A trip into the projects might yield a bag of weed, or you might get robbed. There were flyers all over school warning the students to stay clear of the hood.

The frat house that the party was held in was only a few blocks away, so the girls decided to walk. They endured cat calls and come-ons from passing cars as well as pedestrians. Jackie enjoyed the attention, but seeing that her friend was oblivious to it, she ignored it as well.

Cameisha was focused. She couldn't wait for Curt to see her dressed up a little. She sashayed seductively as they walked by a storefront window. A pleased smile spread on her face when she saw her sexy reflection.

"So, what's his name?" Jackie asked when she saw it.

"Who?" Meisha demanded, embarrassed at being seen through. Usually she pretended to be cool and hard like her mentor, Sincerity, back in the Bronx, but this Curt . . .

Jackie laughed knowingly. "Whoever got you strutting and smiling, that's who."

"I'm saying though . . . I mean, he cute but, feel me?" Cameisha said, trying to make sense of it herself. "I mean, he got a girl so . . ."

In a classic 'speak of the devil' moment, Curt and Arnell were out front as the girls arrived.

"So, I was like Prada or Gucci? Prada or Gucci? Then I just said you know what? Give me both. I mean who can make a decision like that?" Arnell bantered on incessantly as Curt pretended to listen.

He smiled and nodded as if he cared about her trivial matters because some pussy was at the end. Men will endure all kinds of hardship and inane conversation for some ass.

Curt's expression changed into a 'damn, she fine' frown when he saw Cameisha and Jackie. Arnell saw it and turned around to see who or what stole her attention. She absolutely had to be the center of attention at all times, so sharing was bad enough—sharing with Ms. Ragamuffin was too much.

"Hmp!" She huffed even though she had to admit the girl was cute. Of course, she wouldn't admit any such thing, so she stormed off to find her cronies.

Curt didn't even notice her departure as he went to greet Cameisha.

"Mmm, look at this one here!" Jackie moaned lustfully as Curt approached to meet them.

"That's him." Meisha giggled girlishly.

"Hey, ladies," Curt greeted plurally even though he was only talking to Cameisha.

"Hey," she sang coyly, causing Jackie to snicker.

"Anyway, I'm about to grab a . . . get me a . . . okay bye," Jackie said, excusing herself. It was a waste of breath because neither of them heard her.

As usual, Jackie caused a stir when she walked in the party. The unusually dark girl was unusually pretty, and the dim lighting added mystery. A frat boy named Logan was the first one out the blocks and reached her ahead of all competition.

He said, "Hey." She said, "Hey." He offered her a drink, and she said, "Sure."

Logan led her over to the other punch bowl as his date raping buddies smiled knowingly. He ladeled an ample amount of the concoction as Jackie held the glass. He watched eagerly as she lifted it to her lips for a sip.

"Mmm," Jackie lied as she sipped the super sweet drink. The potent mixture had a pound of sugar to mask the 190 proof liquor and date rape drugs.

"Un uh, drink up," Logan goaded, knowing the G14B all molly mixture would have her down for whatever. Unconscious girls never say 'no' or 'I don't do that'.

The servile girl was lifting the cup to her mouth to comply until she spotted trouble. There was Arnell and her girls marching towards the front door. She quickly handed the spiked drink back to the sexual predator and followed them outside.

"Drink?" Logan smiled and offered the next girl who wandered by.

"Sure, thanks!" the bubbly co-ed cheered. She tossed it back to please him and became a statistic.

****

"Thank you." Cameisha giggled at yet another compliment.

He was laying it on thick and was on his way to getting some pussy. She wouldn't have fucked him tonight, but once a woman decided to fuck you, you're in as long as you didn't fuck it up. It was all going so well until the liquid hit her.

"Take a cold shower, Miss Ragamuffin!" Arnell shouted as she tossed a twenty-ounce cup of draft beer on her.

Cameisha had a Big Bessie flashback and attacked. She was on Arnell's ass so quickly, she or her friends had no time to react. Not that the sheltered divas could fight anyway. In their world, a ratchet girl was a chick who didn't own her own car. In their world, you could throw beer on someone and not get your ass kicked. Too bad they weren't in that world because this was brutal.

The first blow closed Arnell's eye swollen shut. The one that closely followed gave her a matching set. Next was a busted beak that bloodied the diva's designer shirt. Meisha tried her best to knock her teeth down her throat with her next flurry of punches. Good thing the cops showed up. Good for Arnell that is, for Meisha not so much.

"What's going on here?" the first officer asked despite the obvious.

"She attacked me!" Arnell shouted, skipping to the middle. She, of course, left out the provocation that led to it.

The cop took one look at the battered girl and took her word for it. He turned to Meisha and removed his cuffs.

"Turn around, you're under arrest," he demanded.

"Me? She started it!" Cameisha shouted. She was ready to punch him in his mouth, too, but shook it off.

"Aww, man!" she whined as the cuffs clicked on her wrists. "Jack, I got some cash in one of my shoeboxes. Come get me!"

"Okay, chica, just hold tight. I'm coming." Jackie shouted as her friend was led away. It broke her heart seeing the tears streaming down her face. She rushed back to the dorm to retrieve bail money.

"Did you find something?" Cynthia pleaded, seeing Jackie rush back in.

Jackie just sucked her teeth and continued her mission. She never violated her friend's space by going through her belongings. Even now with permission, it felt wrong. She found a little more than just the cash.

After being booked, printed, and photographed, Cameisha was given five hundred dollar bail and placed into a holding cell to wait for it to be paid.

"Ugh!" Cameisha grunted when the aroma of fifty women of different social, racial, and hygienic backgrounds cramped in a small room with no air rushed into her life. She held her breath for as long as she could but was forced to breath to live.

A scan of the room gave a wide variety of women accused with a wide variety of crimes. A schoolteacher caught fucking a student, a church secretary caught buying dope with money from the collection plate, a young girl who stabbed a flirtatious boyfriend, and, of course, a slew of prostitutes. Well, actually half were prostitutes; the other half just dressed like prostitutes. It was months away from Halloween, but they wore whore costumes.

The ladies of the night came in different sizes and shapes: old, young, big, and small. A crew of young whores all looking like Nicki Minaj yapped way too loudly for the small space, hoping someone would complain so they could jump on them. They glared dangerously at Meisha as she scanned the room. Not wanting any more trouble, she quickly found a seat.

"Debbie," a broke down old whore greeted as Meisha took a seat next to her on the concrete bench. She offered a smile then remembered it was in her pocket. She retrieved her dentures and popped them in before trying again.

"Meisha." Cameisha laughed.

"What you in fo'?" Debbie asked, sounding like an old prison movie.

"Disorderly conduct. This bitch threw beer on me, so I whooped her ass for her," she replied proudly.

"'Bout some man I bet you. I bet if you dug under the surface, every bitch in here behind some man," Debbie lamented correctly. The same held true over in the males' holding cell too.

"Well, she was just mad 'cause her man like me," Cameisha defended.

"Well, you see what beating her up got you. If you really wanted to get her back, you shoulda just fucked her man," Debbie said plainly. "The bumps and bruises gone heal. Fuck her man, she'll never get over that!"

Cameisha paused to absorb the licentious advice. She was already thinking about having sex with Curt, but she could get back as well. The thought of that sweet reverse sent a tingle between her legs and pulled her mouth into a sinister smile.

"You laughing at me, bitch?" a young hooker in an electric blue wig that matched her tights demanded. For some reason, she thought a clownish, orange-colored mini dress and six-inch heels went well.

"I guess so." Cameisha sighed and stood up to fight. She had already averted her eyes from her when she walked in as a sign of submission. That's all they were getting out of her.

"Oh, so I'm funny?" the prostitute asked, stepping forward. In truth, she was madder at herself than the cute college kid. If not for her own fucked up decisions in life, she could have went to college herself.

"No, you're sad. This ass whooping gone be funny," Meisha said, reverting back to her southern accent.

The crew of hookers followed their leader, ready to join the fray. Debbie stood up to help her new friend, but luckily, the situation was averted.

"Cameisha Forrest!" a guard called as he opened the cell door. "You made bail."

The process to get out of the jail was almost as long as the one getting in—proof that it's easier to stay out of trouble than to get out of trouble. An hour after being called, she was finally free.

"Gurl, am I happy to see you!" Meisha cheered when she saw Jackie waiting in the room used for waiting. She rushed over and wrapped her in a bear hug.

"No problem, ma, you know I'll do anything for you," Jackie said sincerely. She was what's known as a down ass bitch, a rider. Contrary to popular belief, that type of female is rarer than a four leaf clover.

As they left and strolled home, Cameisha filled her friend in on her jailhouse adventures. Jacke wanted to wait on the prostitutes to make bail to see what they were talking about.

"Yo! That chick is lumped the fuck up! Both her eyes are shut." Jackie laughed then got serious. "Sup with the hammer yo?"

Jackie could have bonded her out a little sooner if she hadn't come across that gun. She couldn't help but pick it up and instantly felt its power. Her mind flashed to her Jack and Ill days.

"Okay see, that's um, well," Cameisha stammered from the embarrassment. She felt the same way a woman felt when her stash of dildos was uncovered.

"It's cool, ma, like I told you, I been around the block a couple times myself.

"Oh yeah, Jack and Ill." Cameisha cracked up. She still couldn't buy this timid woman as that notorious killer.

"Anyway, you should beat that bitch's ass again," Jackie announced as they reached the dorm.

"For what? And get locked up again or kicked out of school! Naah, I got something else in mind. Something she'll never get over!" Cameisha said with a wicked grin.

"You guys score? Did you find anything?" their pothead neighbor begged as soon as they hit the hallway.

It was at that moment she decided to get a pack, nothing too serious, a pound or two to flip. Yeah right! She was just like Daddy.

Chapter 7

"Oh hey, Curt, Ki-Ki-Ki." Cameisha giggled to her reflection. She then turned sideways in the mirror to view all that ass poking out in her skintight jeans.

"You stoopid!" Jackie laughed, shaking her head at her friend's antics. Seeing Meisha so out of character amused her until she figured it out. "Ooooh, oooh! I know what you're up to!"

"Moi? I'm not up to anything," Meisha replied coyly, batting her eyes.

"Litte girl, please. You 'bout to fuck her man."

"Shole is." She laughed. "Bitch think she all that, and I'm 'bout to show her. Plus, that nigga is fine!"

"He is that. Shit, I could use some wood my damn self," Jackie added fondly.

"Ain't yo' fast ass had enough for one semester?"

"No, I mean, for real. Like a real boyfriend," Jackie replied, killing the adage of not being able to miss what you never had.

Both girls paused at the prospect of a real boyfriend. Jackie only knew Ill Will and the verbal, physical, and mental abuse he offered. Meisha didn't fare much better since her first love gave her the clap, beat her up, and robbed her. He had a lovely funeral though.

Maybe Curt could be the one? Perhaps they could fall in love, marry, have kids. The thought pasted a wide smile on her face and heart.

"Welp, I'm out," Jackie announced, breaking the silence. She collected her books and rushed off to class.

Cameisha wasn't too far behind her. She tussled her hair to make it look the picture on the cover and headed out the door. All her practice conversation went out the window when she stumbled across Curt earlier than planned.

He had just dropped off a freshman at the dorm. She stumbled past disoriented and limping from a rough night of rough sex. He and Meisha locked eyes just before he pulled off.

"Well, if it ain't Floretta Mayweather," he joked then flashed that pussy magnet smile of his. It worked before and was working now.

"Who?" Cameisha barked with a frown at the boxing reference. The bright girl was an expert on everything that interested her but in total darkness to most everything else, boxing especially.

"Anyway, hop in let me take you to class."

"I can walk," Meisha quipped but slid in the passenger's side anyway. With so many eyes seeing her get in his car, her mission was complete because the rumor mill would say they were fucking.

Curt got an eyeful of that round ass when she got in. He made up his mind that he had to have it. He was the Malcom X of vagina and would get it by any means necessary.

"You need to let me take you to dinner," he offered as they rode.

"What about your girlfriend; she coming too?" Meisha shot back with faked attitude.

"Who? Oh, Arnell took the rest of the semester off," he replied, leaving out the why. The vain girl couldn't be seen with the black eyes, lumps, and bruises Cameisha gave her.

"Sorry about that, girl stuff." She giggled like a girl about beating her like a man.

"Anyway, dinner?" he offered again. He knew a lof of college girls would fuck for food. Some were fucking on the strength, so a man was a come up. If they played hard to get, he would just fix them a drink.

"Okay," Cameisha agreed and did the giggle she had practiced all morning.

****

"You gone get the door?" Jackie asked, snapping Meisha from her daydreaming of Curt.

"And he's a gentleman," she said, hopping off her bed. Most niggas just pulled up front and let most chicks come down. Most nights cars lined the curb like taxis at the airport.

"Wow!" Curt exclaimed at the sight of Cameisha in a low-cut but long white summer dress. She had even pinned a white flower in her hair but couldn't wait to show him the white bra and thong underneath.

"Wow to you, too." She smiled, leaning in for a Hollywood-type hug, lifting a leg in the air.

Curt took advantage of the hug to give Jackie a once-over. Seeing her big black thighs in her tiny shorts got her added to his hit list. Of course, he heard she was fucking, so why not. After Cameisha that is.

"Hey, um . . ." Curt said, pretending not to know Jackie's name.

Cameisha went for it and made the formal introductions. "Jackie, Curt, Curt, Jackie." She giggled again, causing Jackie to frown. Or was it Curt?

"Hey, Jackie. You should let me introduce you to my buddy Santana," Curt offered. He and Santana often ran trains on freshman fresh out the box.

"Number eighty-four!" Jackie gushed excitedly. She—just like every other girl on campus—knew Mark Santana.

The six-foot-one wide receiver was plain gorgeous. He was almost as dark as Jackie but had a head full of curly hair . . . good hair. No girlfriend, but had a reputation with the ladies. It wasn't all good though.

"Yep, that's the one. Good friend of mine. Heres his number," he said, handing her the digits. "Be sure to tell him I gave you the number."

"Okay!" Jackie cheered.

She called him the second the couple walked out of the door. He was busy but gave her a few minutes. By the end of the conversation, Jackie was dreaming of little black curly-headed babies.

Curt and Cameisha walked a few blocks to a nearby soul food restaurant. It was home-cooking at its best since it was actually a house converted into a restaurant. They offered good down home Southern soul food just like Cameisha had as a child and dearly missed.

He laid it on pretty thick over dinner. It was the usual say anything to get some pussy stuff men say to get some pussy. She was going for it and made up her mind to fuck him. He earned himself the coveted coochie coupon.

"That was delicious." Curt sighed as they left the restaurant.

"It was," she agreed and slipped her hand into his for security.

The neighborhood was dangerous since the local thugs made a living robbing the college kids. They were eating pretty well from stolen watches, rings, and tablets. For some reason, they never stole any e-readers. Go figure. Too bad they weren't smart enough to steal those expensive ass textbooks. A used book had a higher resale value than a stolen smartphone but the dumb thugs didn't know better.

Cameisha was the first to notice two men moving in the shadows as they walked. Had she been alone, she would have crossed the street, but since she was with a man, she squeezed his hand. She hoped they could walk by with no problem, but when the ski mask came down, when the guns came out, she remembered hers sitting in a shoebox.

"Break yourself!" the shorter of the two robbers screamed in a shrill voice that irritated more than intimidated.

The second man stood back with his gun by his side as if he were supervising. Cameisha thought about disarming the short guy nervously waving a small pistol back and forth. Her only dilemma was would she be able to shoot the other one before he got a shot off? Good thing she was with a man.

"Help! Help! Somebody help!" a woman screamed.

Cameisha was just as surprised as the stick-up kids to see the woman was Curt. He snatched his hand away from her, shoved her at the robbers, and took off running.

"The fuck?" Meisha frowned, watching him tear off down the street.

"Hell naw!" The leader of the two laughed.

"Come off that purse and that watch, bitch," the short one yelled, resuming the robbery.

"Bitch?" Meisha growled. She was already hot about her date running off and being robbed, but bitch?

"Dats right, bitch," he repeated, moving closer. Too close and paying for it.

Cameisha grabbed his arm to keep him from aiming at her. She spun inside delivering an elbow to his mouth that knoced out a tooth. She took the gun away as he scrambled for his gold tooth. She immediately turned the gun on the other robber, but he never raised his. Instead, he raised the ski mask from his face. Cameisha blinked rapidly, trying to process the pretty thug standing in front of her.

He stood average height and weight and had her same golden complexion. The street lights made his hazel eyes glow. He cracked a half-smile, showing half of his gold teeth.

"You think I let that fool put bullets in that gun?" he asked in a voice so deep it sounded like it belonged to a much older man. It had a raspiness of years of blunt smoking that only added to its appeal.

Cameisha turned the gun to the other robber and pulled the trigger five times; one for every letter in the word bitch. Big Shawty, as he was called, ducked and rolled away having forgotten the gun wasn't loaded.

"Now go in that purse of yours and hand me a pen and paper," the lead robber demanded.

Since he had a gun, Cameisha complied and handed over a pen and paper. She watched curiously as he scribbled on it and handed it back before turning and walking off.

"She got my gun, Dro!" Big Shawty whined as he rushed to catch up.

"So, get it from her." He laughed and kept stepping.

"Yeah right, Pedro!" Cameisha huffed, looking at the name and number on the paper. She tore it in two and tossed it to the pavement.

Right before getting back to the dorm, Cameisha chucked the little gun in a dumpster and went inside. She vowed then to keep her own gun on her at all times.

Chapter 8

"Girl, no he didn't?" Jackie laughed as Cameisha filled her in on her date from the night before.

"The hell he didn't! Nigga screamed like a bitch and left me." Meisha laughed even though she was steaming. Instead of giving him some ass, she wanted to kick his. "Them niggas could have raped or killed me!" she lamented. "Oh, oh! Then the cute one tried to give me his number!"

Jackie frowned. "Cute one?"

"I aint say cute!" Meisha shot back. She was embarrassed at liking the thug, among other things.

"And anyway, I spoke to Santana," Jackie sang like a school girl.

"And?"

"And, I don't think I'ma fuck with him since him and Curt so cool," she said sadly. A glance at the clock showed ten till class and off she went.

Cameisha's alone time was cut short by a knock on the door. She vowed that if it was another weed junky searching for weed, they were getting their ass kicked. Desperate potheads roamed the halls in search of pot nonstop. Instead, when she snatched the door open she saw . . .

"Curt? Fuck you want?" she demanded and waited—waited instead of closing the door in his face. A mistake she would pay for very soon.

"Girl, are you okay? Where did you?" he asked and hugged her protectively.

"Where did I go? Nigga, you the one who took off and left me," she said confused. He did leave me, didn't he? He does smell good, don't he? Is that his dick I feel?

"I ran back to my car to get my gun. Time I got back you were gone," he said, offering his eyes to ease the lies. "Oh and I caught up with them two."

42

"You did?" Meisha asked hopefully.

This was the nibble fishermen feel when they get a bite. Since he had her on the line, he went on and reeled her in.

"And you screamed like a bi . . . eh, like a wo . . . I mean, why were you screaming?" she begged because that needed explaining as well.

"To distract them so you could get away. Trust me, those guys won't be robbing anyone else anytime soon!" he said confidently.

"Thank you, thank you," Meisha said, bouncing. She pulled back into the embrace. She was so happy he wasn't a pussy that she decided to give him some pussy.

When he stiffened against her, she leaned into it. Curt pushed the issue by palming her ass and pushing his tongue inside of her mouth. When he felt her knees buckle, he knew he had her.

"So, you wanna go out again tonight?" he asked, licking his lips.

"Nope. I wanna stay in tonight," she replied and helped him lick his lips.

****

"Guess I'll call Santana," Jackie sighed when Meisha told her of her plans for the evening. She sighed as if she didn't want to sex the sexy man who had all the young girls fucked up. Only Jackie was no young girl. She was going to fuck him because she wanted to.

"Or you can just go to the library and study. I mean, I wouldn't want you doing anything you don't want to do," Cameisha said, calling her bluff.

"Nah, I'm cool. I'll call him." She laughed and did just that.

Both girls showered and prepared for their separate booty calls. Jackie slipped into a red thong and bra and topped it with baggy sweats. No need in all the extras, she was going to fuck.

Cameisha went with black boy shorts and a wife beater with no bra. A Japanese style robe served as a gift wrap. She was all set to lose her virginity again. According to her, the first time didn't count because Tay turned out to be some bullshit.

At nine-thirty on the dot, a firm knock announced Curt's presence . . . and he had a present. Jackie opened the door, gave him half a smile, and slipped past.

"Hey, you. You look great," he said to her and the pretty thighs exposed under the short robe.

"You, too." Cameisha giggled and tippy-toed for a kiss. "Come on in, I'll take that."

Curt sat on the bed while Cameisha put the wine coolers in glasses. She purposely bent over to let him see some ass cleavage, but he was too busy opening the small vial of liquid to slip her.

****

"Shit better be worth it," Jackie said to herself as she hoofed the ten blocks over to Santana's apartment.

Since it was her who offered to link up with him, he told her to fall through instead of going to pick her up. Supply and demand, you know. The future pro used some of his illegal, under the table money for a Lexus and off-campus pussy palace. Jackie climbed the stairs and rang the bell.

"Damn!" Jackie and Santana exclaimed at the same time at the sight of each other.

He was shocked to see just how pretty she was close up, and she was shocked at what he had on. A pair of gym shorts was the only cloth separating him from being naked. Jackie named each muscle group starting with pecs, triceps, abs, and the huge bulge in his shorts. That, of course, was the dick muscle.

"I got the stuff you asked for," Jackie said, handing him the bag and feeling some kinda way about it.

To further try her up, Santana had her stop at the store for a bottle of wine and box of condoms. It was a player's way of asking, "Are we fucking?"

"Thanks, pick a movie while I poor us a glass."

Jackie bit her tongue about the movie and went to his vast collection. If she wanted to watch a movie, she could have stayed home. She came for sex. When she peeped a nice-sized stack of unlabed DVDs, she knew they had to be the porn stash. She was about to ask about it, but when she looked back, there was Santana emptying a small vial in one of the glasses. Hers she assumed.

Her first thought was to kill him. Go into his well-equipped kitchen, grab a knife, and cut his throat. See, that's how killers think—murder first, talk later. They found conversation with the dead easier. A better thought came to mind and put a devious smile on her face.

"How's this baby?" she asked, holding up the Preacher's Wife DVD. It was appropriate since the theme for the night was don't get mad, get even.

"Fine." He smiled backed. It's not like he gave a fuck what she picked. She would be asleep a few minutes into it anyway. He would be into her a minute after that.

The funny thing was that most of the girls he date raped would have fucked him anyway. Only most of them wouldn't have been down for all the extra shit he was going to put them through: the filming, the friends, etc.

When they snuggled up on the sofa, Santana passed her her glass and pressed play on the remote. He watched with glee as she raised it to her mouth.

"Ooh! Grab my chips out the bag, please," she pleaded, touching his stomach.

"Sure," he replied and rushed over to where he sat the bag. He was quick, being a wide receiver and all, but Jackie was quicker when she swapped the glasses.

"Thanks." She smiled and took a sip. "Toast?"

"To us!" Santanta cheered like the cheerleaders he date raped and drained his glass.

Jackie leaned into him and watched trifling Teresa on the screen. *What a waste*, she thought to herself, feeling his erection grow against her back. Ten minutes into the movie, he was yawning and blinking, rapidly trying to stay awake.

"Are you okay, honey?" Jackie teased knowingly.

"Um, I um, just . . ." he stammered just like his many victims did between yawns.

The football player was strong, but date rape drugs were stronger. A few minutes later, he was out like a light. When he woke up the next day, he wasn't going to remember a thing. Just like his victims.

****

"Damn, girl, look at you!" Curt marveled as he stripped Cameisha's under garments off. Of course, she didn't giggle or thank him since she was sound asleep.

After fondling her firm breasts and freshly-shaved vagina, he was ready. He stripped his own clothing off and turned the camera in his phone on to record the action. The filming began in her mouth as he ran his erection in and out. He stopped just short of climax and entered her box. A few strokes later, he filled it up as he climaxed. After a brief rest, he was ready to go again.

"One hole left," he announced to the intended future audience and flipped Meisha on her stomach.

****

"Well, let's see whatcha working with," Jackie mused as she tugged the shorts off the sleeping athlete.

"Dang!" She frowned at the nice-sized dick that fell out.

She came to fuck him and would have had a ball riding it. After playing with it for longer than she really should have, she sat it down and got to work. Jackie found what she was looking for in the bathroom and got to work.

"First, let's do something with this hair," She said, turning the clippers on.

His curly locks came off cleanly with each pass. It was just like shearing a sheep as she shaved him bald. Next to go was the mustache and goatee. His eyebrows and pubic hair came off after that.

"Now, let's have a look at this wardrobe," Jackie announced. She retrieved a harp pair of scissors from the knife set on the kitchen counter and went to his walk-in closet.

"None of this will do." She laughed aloud and set out to destroy everything inside. Every pair of pants, shirts, shoes, and belts were cut to ribbons.

The sheets and comforter went next before she got started on the contents of the dressers. She was actually winded by the time she finished cutting everything that could be cut.

"Still wanna watch a movie? Me pick?" Santana replied in snores. She picked one of the unmarked DVDs and popped it in. "Let's see what you were going to do to me."

Jackie literally felt her blood began to boil as she watched young girls being raped by Santana and his friends. One freshman lived down the hall from her. She remembered seeing her coming in one morning looking confused and disoriented. She now knew why watching three football players taking turns in her mouth and vagina.

"I should kill your fucking ass," Jackie growled down at the man. Her thought ran from cutting his throat to setting the place on fire. "Nahh, I got something better for you. Your ass is going to jail!"

Jackie collected the discs and poured water in all thirty thousand dollars worth of his electronics. She then went into the kitchen to destroy everything within, including the food. As she grabbed his car keys from the table, his phone began to vibrate. Since she was taking it, too, she decided to read the incoming text.

"Just fucked this bitch nine ways to Sunday. I need to stop over and fuck that black bitch too," Curt texted.

"Oh no!" Jackie screamed and rushed out. She jumped in the Lexus and sped towards campus.

Jackie pulled into the notoriously dangerous gas station near school and got out. Two goons saw her pull up and rushed over to car jack her. To their surprise, she left it running and took off. She ran the rest of the way to school, into the dorm, up the stairs, into the room and . . .

"Oh no!" she cried at the sight of her friend.

Cameisha was sprawled out naked on top of her bed. This was something the private girl would never do. Her eyes partially opened, just like Santana's, were from the drug. Jackie cleaned the semen off of her face and body and covered her up.

"Come on and get some," she texted back to Curt and hit the closet. Once she found what she was looking for, she ran the ten blocks back to Santana's.

Had Curt looked up, he would have seen Jackie enter the open apartment just as he pulled up. Instead, he parked and ran up the steps. Curt knocked on the door eagerly in a rush to get at Jackie too.

Jackie pulled the door from behind it, so he didn't see her when he stepped in. Instead, he saw the ransacked apartment and his shaved friend. A confused frown spread on his face, and he died wearing it.

Two shots into his temple from the forty meant a closed casket. His family was going to have to pick a picture of him from happier times to blow up and put next to the casket. Maybe one with him smiling because he certainly wasn't smiling now.

"I wish I could kill your fuck ass again," Jackie told him as she took his keys and phone.

She parked Curt's car in that same gas station and got the same results. A second pair of thieves rode off with his car along with a murder weapon.

Chapter 9

Jackie watched Cameisha stir awake the next afternoon with a heavy heart. She knew she had to tell her only friend she had been victimized, just wasn't sure how. Maybe she would start with the good news of Curt's death and Santana's arrest. Of course, he would beat the murder charge, but all of those sex tapes meant he was going to jail. Dumb ass documented hundreds of hours of date rapes that would be used against him. He was his own star witness.

"The fuck yo? My head is booming!" Meisha groaned as she sat up in bed.

Jackie sat back and watched her do the math as she put two and two together. An intense frown washed over her face as she felt her body.

"Yo, I think my stuff is sore, my . . . I think this nigga raped me? I'm all sore and can't remember shit!" she complained.

"Think, Meisha, did he fix you a drink? Did he give you anything?" Jackie urged.

"Um, he came over, we had wine coolers, and . . ." Cameisha recalled and leapt from the bed.

She dashed into the bath and under the shower in a flash. Even though she never used a douche before, she grabbed the box that sat on the counter. After reading the directions, she inserted it and flushed out the evidence left behind. She didn't know it yet, but it wasn't needed anyway. Jackie had already tried, convicted, sentenced, and executed the rapist.

Cameisha was so intent on murder she didn't bother drying off. She burst naked from the bathroom and went straight for her closet. When her frantic search came up empty, she turned to Jackie.

"Where my hammer at?" she asked, holding the empty box.

"I threw it away," Jackie explained. Instead of a gun, she extended her hand containing a small white pill in her palm.

"Fuck you mean, you threw it away? What the hell is that?" Meisha barked. She was equally confused by the answer as she was the pill.

"Well, the pill is the morning-after pill. Just in case that bastard ain't use no rubber," she explained, hoping not to have to admit to murder. Now that's a hard pill to swallow.

Cameisha snatched the pill and tossed it back into her throat using spit to swallow. "Now where my gun?"

"I, um, I shot Curt in his head with it, so it became a murder weapon. Murder weapons get dumped, so that's what I did!" she said flatly.

"You kilt Curt? Back on that Jack and Ill shit, I see! This ain't the time to play. I ne . . ." Meisha spazzed until being cut off by a frantic knock on the door.

"Did y'all hear? Did y'all hear!?" Cynthia begged, hoping she was first to spread the bad news. Black people—well, niggas—are like news reporters and love to get the scoop.

"Hear what?" Both Cameisha and Jackie shouted. Caught up in the drama she repeated.

Cynthia wasn't just a drama major, she was a drama queen. Everything with her was a Broadway production.

"Curt dead; Santana got locked up; y'all got weed?" she laid out in one breath.

"No!!" Both girls shouted at the desperate little pothead.

Cynthia shrugged like 'oh well'. She figured she may as well try since she had the floor.

"So, they say Santana and dem was raping girls!" Cynthia announced. "See, that's why I do like I do. Niggas ain't good for but two things: weed and dick. I'll smoke a nigga's whole sack, get me a nut, and be gone."

"I feel you," Cameisha said sadly. Sad part was that she really did feel her. In the state that she was in being a hoe sounded quite reasonable. "If you do find some weed let me know."

"You smoke?" Jackie asked incredulously. In the couple of months they had lived together, she had never seen her use anything harder than a wine cooler, which is only slightly harder than mouthwash.

"If and when I feel like it, I do, and I feel like it," Cameisha quipped.

****

"This is a dime sack!" Meisha screeched at the gram of ugly, brown weed her ten bucks purchased.

"Yup, that's all Turbo had, that and some twenties that ain't even twice this," Cynthia replied just as hot.

The nerdy little dealer was making out quite well selling what little weed he could come across. The local projects were filled with drugs but far too dangerous for the college kids to venture in.

Cynthia and Cameisha smoked both their bags of weed back-to-back and had nothing more than bad breath and a slight headache to show for it. After a few weeks of puffing on bullshit, Cameish decided to act.

Cynthia's 'smoke a nigga's sack and get me a nut' philosophy had begun to sound good, so she thought why not kill two birds with one stone—one thug actually.

Cameisha put the torn pieces of paper together and it spelled Pedro. It was written in the chicken scratch of a third grader, but she wasn't in search of a tutor. She laughed and shook her head at the memory of tearing up the number, throwing it down, only to pick it back up. God made her work for it, too, by sending a wind that blew one piece under a car.

At first she blocked her number when she called, which was odd considering what she had in mind. She planned on giving up the goodies but would rather he didn't have her phone number. A quick one-night stand would take the edge off and be done with it. When the call went straight to voicemail, she sighed and hung up. Then sighed and called back. The dope girl knew dope boys don't take calls from private numbers. This time she didn't block her number and got an answer.

"Who dis?" the gruff voice replied, sending a tingle to her lonely private parts. He frowned at the strange area code that could have been from the moon for all he knew. Have him tell it New York was just as far.

"This the girl you tried to rob," she said curtly.

Pedro paused for a second since they had robbed quite a few girls but smiled remembering only giving his number to one. "Sup, lil mama?"

"Tryna find some trees," Cameisha said, revealing half her mission.

"You tryna shop or you wanna hang out?"

"Um, both I guess. Some kids here want a couple of sacks, but what you talking?"

"Shit, I can come through and scoop you so we can chill," he offered hopefully. Chill meant fuck in his world, so when she said okay, he knew it was going down.

Cameisha felt a twinge of 'girl, what the fuck are you doing?' but didn't act on it. She was sinking into that black hole called 'niggas aint shit syndrome'. If a good man didn't come along soon, she could spend years knowingly fucking with dudes she knew were no good for her. It's a vicious cycle, and before you know it, you're a lonely old woman. The woman who constantly says, "I can do bad all by myself", usually does just that: bad all by herself.

She found herself standing out on the curb along with the other girls niggas didn't respect enough to park and call on properly. When a custom boxy Chevy sitting high on twenty-four inch rims turned onto the block, she knew it was her date. If a good man didn't come into the picture soon, she may be doomed.

Pedro was not a good man. In fact, he was a piece of shit. He grew up a few blocks away in the same projects he still lived in. The grandmother who raised him never told him that one of the skinny crack whores who patrolled the area was actually his mother. He sold dope to her on plenty of occasions as a result. Good thing he wasn't the type to trick with geek monsters.

That's not to say he was very proficient as a dealer—he wasn't. Ninety percent of the males in the projects sold dope. It was a right of passage, just as was prison and early deaths. Pedro lived to ball and fucked up his re-up more often than not. That's why him and his side-kick, the five-one, two hundred pound Big Shawty, turned to stick ups.

"Thought you wasn't gone call?" Pedro said, making it sound like a question as Cameisha slid into the passenger's side.

"Well, I usually don't mess with niggas after they rob me," she shot back.

Pedro showed her his gold teeth and dimples in reply and put the donk in gear. Cameish stole a glance at him in his ATL hood swagger and confirmed the fact that he was getting some. So what if he thought she was easy since she wasn't. It was just like Cynthia said: smoke his weed and get a nut. One time affair and business as usual tomorrow.

"My people at my spot, so I got us a room," Pedro announced as they rode. By his people he meant his grandmother, several cousins, and two of his kids.

The sexy hood nigga had six kids by five hood rats and two more by college girls just like Cameisha. Luckily for those kids, their mothers retreated back to whence they came, giving them a decent shot at a decent life. Hopefully clean air, good schools, and proper upbringing could overcome the cum he passed in his DNA.

To sweeten the offer, he passed a neatly-rolled blunt and pushed in the car's lighter. Cameisha accepted it and was right there when the lighter popped out. She lit it and inhaled deeply. The weed was a good mid-grade from Cali or Mexico, and she savored the taste. A smile spread on her face from the warming glow that is THC. She smoked a quarter of the blunt before passing it to the owner.

Cameisha almost protested when Pedro turned into the parking lot of a rundown motel. It was so shabby it looked like it had never seen better days. A couple skinny crack whores roamed wide-eyed in search of a blast.

"Here we go," he said seductively as he pulled to a stop in front of a room.

Knowing she would back out if she stopped to think, Cameisha shut her brain off and got out. She waited as he fished the room key from a pocket and opened the door. Cameisha winced from the aroma of the room as they walked in.

The tobacco smell she could identify, but it was mixed with cum, blood, sweat, and tears. Still on auto-pilot, she moved forward. Pedro stripped her before removing his clothes. Foreplay was sucking her nipples as he finger fucked her. Once she soaked his fingers sufficiently, he took position between her legs.

Pedro is, was, and always would be a roughneck, and that's exactly how he fucked Cameisha. Her brain came back on once he plunged his thick dick inside of her. She realized he didn't put on a condom, but the in and out felt too good to stop him.

"Girrrll!" He grinned and filled her box as he came. He reiterated by hitting it a couple of more times before finally taking her back to campus.

With a crisp hundred from her purse, Cameisha bought ten ghetto-sized dime bags. That's how it started—just like daddy.

Chapter 10

When the dorm room burst open without a knock, both Cameish and Jackie jumped to their feet and prepared for battle. The local thugs had recently started running in the dorms and doing stick-ups. Both girls wished they still had a gun.

"You got any more? Tell me you have more!" Cynthia pleaded, oblivious to how close she came from getting her ass kicked.

"Nah, you got the last one last time you came," Cameisha lied. Truth was she still had a bag of the good weed but was keeping it for herself.

When she showed Cynthia the weed, she shoved a twenty dollar bill at her, snatched one of the sacks, and fled. Cynthia was no dealer, but as a fledgling addict, she was just as clever. She took the dime bag to her room, rolled a blunt out of it, and made two dimes the size that Turbo sold. Actually, they were a little bigger and sold immediately.

She smoked her free blunt and went back for another, then another, until none were left. The girl still had pinched enough for eight more free blunts, but that wouldn't last the pothead too long.

"Might be over with yo," Meisha said, causing Jackie to twist her lips. "What?"

"Like you ain't going back to see that nigga." She laughed as Cynthia slinked out of the room.

"I'm not!" Meisha shouted indignantly. "One night stand yo. I got mine," she said even though she didn't. Nut or not she did enjoy the sex.

"Please, that nigga had you limping in at two in the morning humming love songs. You going back!"

"I gotta see him to get more weed, but that nigga won't get this pussy. You heard me? He. Will. Not. Get this pussy!"

****

"Get this pussy!" Cameisha heard herself demand Pedro behind her.

That's exactly what he was doing as he delivered textbook back shots. He had a fistful of her curls and the other on her waist holding her in place. He thrust hard solid shots making their skin slapping echo in the sparce room.

This time he took her to his traphouse. The back room was bare except for a mattress on the floor for just this occasion. Maybe if she knew how many skeezers and crack whores had been boned there, she might not have been with it. Might that is, because the bad boy was bringing out the bad girl in her. When the first orgasm of her young life shook her world, she was done. Love has a close cousin named whipped, be it pussy-whipped or dick-whipped, the symptoms are the same.

"Mmm, I gotta get back," Cameisha moaned but made no attempt to move. She really didn't want to go but didn't want to hear Jackie's 'told you so'. Still, if Pedro told her to stay she would have. If he wanted to hit again, he could have.

"Yeah, I gotta make some moves myself," he said, pulling himself out of her. Not only did he have some trapping to do but a date with a baby momma later.

"You still need that?"

"Um, yeah," Meisha replied sadly. She was in brief mourning from him taking his dick out of her life. "Let me get an ounce."

"What you doing with all this weed?" he asked and lit a blunt.

"Sell it! Them kids at my school smoke more weed than a lil bit."

"Sho nuff?" Pedro asked and passed the blunt. The question was the rhetorical type since he knew the answer.

All the thugs knew the college kids smoked hella weed, pills, coke, and everything else, but getting one on the inside wasn't easy. For one, the kids weren't street kids and often got caught. Once they did get caught, eleven out of ten times they were going to snitch. The judges would give them a slap on the wrist but knock the local's head off for corrupting them.

"Tell you what?" Pedro said as the wheels spun in his head. "Why don't I just give you some work, and you can sell for me!"

"It's better to be the boss than be bossed." Her father's advice echoed in her head.

"Nah, I'm cool. I'll just pay upfront but make sure I only shop with you," she replied.

"Aight, seventy-five an ounce," he shot back. The sting of being rejected could be heard in his voice, but she missed it. Had she paid attention, she would have heard the snake hiss.

She did frown at the high price though. It made her look down at the small bed and think that what had just took place should at least call for fair market price. The dope girl knew that grade of weed didn't go for more than fifty bucks an ounce. But since she stood to make two hundred at school she said, "Okay."

The trap house was in full swing when the couple emerged from the back room. A young dealer rushed a young crackhead in as soon as they walked out. Two thugs sat at the kitchen table cutting and bagging crack while two others competed in a video game. One of them lost it along with one of his virtual lives when he saw Cameisha.

"Oh hell naw! What that bitch doing here?" Big Shawty demanded minus one gold tooth.

"Chill," Pedro ordered as he restrained Meisha from going after him.

"That's right, I said bitch, bitch! Don't like it, bitch?" Shawty taunted.

Cameisha just smiled and nodded. She would be a bitch for now but made a mental appointment to get that mouth first chance she got.

"Bitch, bitch, bitch, bitch," followed her out the door.

****

"Okay, check it. Here go twenty dimes. Keep four for yourself and bring me back one sixty," Cameisha explained to Cynthia who was visibly shaking at the sight of so much weed.

"Six! I get six," she said eagerly.

"Okay, six, bring me one forty," Cameisha readily agreed since she knew she tried her with the twenty percent.

"I'll be right back!" she practically shouted and scooped up the bags. In a flash, she was out the door.

"Ay-yo, that bitch a fucking junky," Jackie lamented as soon as she left.

"She cool yo," Meisha replied, trying to fool herself. In truth, she felt the same way. The pretty, young freshman was fucking for weed already, no telling what she would do if she got hold of anything stronger.

"Can you trust her?" Jackie asked, testing her naivety.

"No, but it's only for a sec. I ain't gone keep selling."

Jackie opened her mouth to say something, but the door opened before she got it out. They both looked at Cynthia harshly for barging in again, but she came bearing gifts.

"Here!" she shouted, shoving a fistful of money at Cameisha. "Count it! It's all there, count it! It's all there, count it!"

Cameisha didn't count it but did look at her watch. The girl was gone for ten minutes and sold out. She felt a sense of dread but still picked up her phone and dialed.

"Sup? I need two more." she told Pedro when he picked up.

That's how it began.

Chapter 11

Through Cameisha, through Cynthia, Pedro was selling a couple of ounces a day in the college. The only problem was he was only a petty dealer himself and couldn't make much money wholesaling ounces. In fact, Cynthia was making more off an ounce than he was. She, of course, smoked hers all up.

More often than not, he either didn't have or couldn't afford to sell Cameisha the weed she needed. Sometimes he could sell her some dimes to flip, sometimes not. He always fucked her though. Night after night she compromised herself for an orgasm.

"Can you do anything with these?" Pedro asked after a vigorous bout of sex that left them both winded. He showed her a handful of pills from his pocket.

"What are they? What do they do?" she asked, picking one up for inspection. "X?"

"Yeah, I know y'all college kids be rolling, so I picked up a bomb for you," he lied. In fact, he got them in a recent burglary.

"I guess they do? Most want weed, you ain't got nothing?" Meisha whined. Not only had the hustle bug hit her, she was getting used to getting high every day.

"Tomorrow, but I'll let you get these for . . . ten for the hundred," he said, calculating how much he could spend at the club. "They go for the dub, so it's a quick double up."

"Okay," Cameisha agreed. The quick flip was hard to pass for a true hustla. She figured she would double her money real quick and then flip that.

Her hopes for one more nut were dashed when Pedro hopped out of the bed and got dressed. She paid him for the pills and squeezed back into her jeans. He drove her back to the school with Big Shawty sulking in the back seat. Pedro demanded that they didn't speak to each other, but they still hated to be in each other's presence.

As usual, Cynthia was in her room pretending to talk to Jackie, waiting on the weed.

"Did you score?" Cynthia yelled, jumping to her feet when Cameisha limped in.

"Did I!" She laughed, referring to getting dicked down real good. "But I ain't got no weed. I'll let you get these for twenty."

"Cool beans!" she cheered, plucked one from her palm and popped it. "Ten bucks, right?"

"Letting them go for twenty," Cameisha replied, still counting on the double up.

"Twenty! For X? Where they do that at?" Cynthia laughed. "Girl ten, fifteen tops in the city."

Meisha frowned, trying to figure out who was lying. On one hand, Cynthia was a crackhead in training, a card carrying member of Future Crackhead of America. She had yet to be introduced to cocaine, but when she did, it would be until death do they part.

Then there was sexy, cool, slimy Pedro on the other hand. Her soul been telling her not to trust him, but he had some good love. If fucking him was wrong, she didn't want to be right.

"Well here, I'm out," Cynthia sang and passed Cameisha a ten dollar bill. She grabbed Jackie's soda from her hand and took a swig to pull the pill down her throat. After passing the bottle back, she turned and left.

"If I find out that bitch lying about how much these go for, I'ma beat that ass," Meisha vowed.

"And if he lying?" Jackie shot back with venom dripping from her fangs. She had been biting her tongue long enough and decided to speak up.

"Fuck that's 'posed to mean?" Meisha shot back defensively. She knew she was slumming but still didn't want to be checked about it. "Don't let me find out you hatin.'"

"Hatin'? Girl, stop! You can do better yo. You a bad bitch and that nigga is a dirt bag. Don't forget how you met him," Jackie replied, bringing it down a notch.

Cameisha was too smart to argue against right but too stubborn to admit wrong. Instead, she dropped the pills in her purse and left the room. It wasn't the first flare-up the couple had, but they were both smart enough to drop it and let it stay dropped. They would agree to disagree and move on.

Her destination was the co-ed dorm a block away. The building was nicknamed the Fertility Clinic because more children were conceived there than some small countries. That is where the resident drug expert lived. The nerdy teen sounded more like a white kid trying to be black than the actual black guy that he was. It was his pretending to be a drug dealer that was about to cost him.

"Ca, ca, ca, c, c," Turbo stuttered upon pulling his door open and seeing Cameisha.

"Cameisha!" she assisted and pushed inside the room.

Turbo swallowed with a big gulp in an attempt to pull himself together. "'Bout time you popped by to see a brother," he said, batting his eyes. He cracked a slanted smile and nodded knowingly.

Cameisha paused to analyze his odd demeanor then frowned when she figured it out. "You think? Boy, stop." She laughed, wiping the smile off his face and breaking his heart. "How much these go for? I'll let you get 'em for twenty."

"Twenty for X? Try ten, but I'm cool," he shot back.

"A'ight, just give me ten a piece for them then," she said, hoping to recoup her money.

"No can do. My man Dro from the projects is selling me ten pounds for eight thousand," he said proudly. "Bout to be the man!"

"Pedro from the projects?" She frowned. They had just had sex, and she knew he didn't have any weed to sell.

She had been trying to get some weight from him for months to satisfy the heavy demand of the college kids. Pedro couldn't come up with more than a few ounces at a time, so where did he get ten pounds from? The petty dealer only dealt paltry amounts of drugs.

"That's the one. We cool like that. Said he's gonna take me to the club with him one day," Turbo said smugly. He had actually pulled the money from his trust fund hoping to flip it and put it back before his mom found out it was gone.

"Look, Turbo, I don't think that's a good idea. I'm going home for Christmas break and can get you weed cheaper than that," she warned.

Pedro was the type to middle-man a deal and add his fee in, but something told Cameisha it was more sinister than that. She put two and two together and got nine.

"Oh, don't be a hater!" Turbo laughed. "I know Cynthia was selling for you! You bitches stole all my customers."

"Tell Pedro I said hey." Cameisha laughed. She passed on beating him up for using the B-word in her direction, knowing he was about to get robbed was payback enough.

Out in the hall she quickly called Pedro's phone. "What you doing? Come back and get me," she blurted when he picked up.

"Can't. I got some shit going on. I'll get at you tomorrow," he drawled and hung up.

Cameisha saw his donk pull up to the building as she crossed the street. A second later, Turbo emerged from the dorm and headed for the car.

"Sup, shawty, you got that?" Pedro asked as Turbo slid into the back seat.

"Eight th . . . uh, stacks," Turbo said proudly.

"A'ight, let's go get that," Pedro said, nodding at Big Shawty in the passenger's seat.

Pedro pulled from the curb and headed towards Cascade Road. He pulled to the park, parked and got out. Turbo naively followed him in to the dark park. He was mentally spending his profits as Shawty slipped behind him and pulled a pistol.

"In the woods?" Turbo asked once they passed the tree line.

"Almost there," Pedro replied, leading him deeper into the woods. "Okay, here we go. Let me get that."

Turbo reached into both pockets and came up with four grand from each. As soon as he handed the cash to Pedro, Big Shawty shot him in the back of his head. His body was still twitching as they left him and walked back to the car. They split the money and hit the club.

Chapter 12

"Y'all got weed!" Cynthia demanded as she barged in the girls' room, waking them both up.

"Why you ain't lock the door!" Jackie yelled over to Cameisha and tossed her pillow.

"Me? You were the last one in," Meisha shot back, sending the pillow with it.

Cynthia watched the verbal volley back and forth, like at a tennis match, as they debated who left the door open. When she couldn't wait anymore, she caught the pillow in mid-air, interrupting the match.

"I need some weed! That damn X had me so horny I played in my coochie all night! I need me a blunt!" she insisted.

"Eww." Jackie frowned and got up to snatch her pillow back. "I do know where your hands have been."

"Go holla at Turbo. He should be straight," Cameisha replied. She took the opportunity to check her phone for traces of Pedro. She both hoped he did and hoped he didn't text or call.

"He dead," Cynthia replied nonchalantly.

"That nigga should have a few pounds over there. I need to hit him my damn self."

"Nah, he dead, dead. Somebody killed him last night, so I know he ain't got no weed."

"What! Yo, that's fucked up," Jackie wailed as tears welled in her eyes.

"Shole is! How we s'posed to get weed now?" Cynthia moaned.

"Get the fuck out!" Cameisha growled. She leapt from the bed and went after Cynthia. "Fuckin' junky bitch!"

Cynthia got the hint and got out of the room before Meisha could get to her. Cameisha locked the door then fell against it crying.

"Oh no," she moaned and slid slowly down the door until she was seated. "He was just a kid."

"I know, baby," Jackie said and joined her on the floor. She held her while she sobbed and rocked. "It's okay, mama."

"Yo, Pedro did that shit!" Cameisha announced, switching gears. The tears stopped instantly as rage pushed sorrow aside. She was now as mad as she was sad.

"Say word! How you know?" Jackie questioned.

"I went to ask him about the X pills last night. He told me he was buying ten pounds of weed from Dro. I saw the money, and I saw him get in the car with him," she recounted.

"Ten pounds? That nigga couldn't get ten damn ounces!" Jackie frowned.

Since they began peddling weed, he stood in the way of them doing business because he wasn't consistent.

"That low budget nigga set him up to rob him. They killed him. I should kill his ass," Meisha whispered.

Jackie was a killer and heard the murderous tone. Only killers spoke like that and only killers could hear it. It was like one of those whistles only dogs hear.

"Chill, ma, he'll get his," Jackie assured her buddy. She was confident since she decided just then to kill him.

"I know he will," Meisha agreed. She, too, had made up her mind to murder him.

****

"You sure you don't wanna come? I'll pay your way and you can stay with us," Cameisha pleaded again as she packed a small tote bag.

"For what? I ain't got no family. Mom Dukes dead and my cousin is some bullshit. Enjoy Christmas with your family; I'll be alright," Jackie replied, hiding the pain hearing the truth caused.

"Mm hm, I bet you will. Probably gone have some nigga in here before I get to the airport!" Meisha laughed.

"Why whatever do you mean?" Jackie laughed coyly.

Her friend had hit the nail on the head because she planned on fucking for Christmas break. She had been a good girl for months, but a grad student had caught her eye. They had been flirting for weeks, and since he was a local, she was staying.

"Okay, bye!" Meisha shouted and took off.

She hated leaving her but couldn't wait to see her grandmother and Sincerity. The thought of Dasia and Aqua crossed her mind, but she quickly dimissed them. They were from her past. She was focused on her future. The cab pulled up to the dorm just as Cameisha stepped outside and off she went.

Later that evening, Jackie prepped for her date. Booty calls don't require much wardrobe, so after a hot shower and pubic hair trim, she slipped on a thong and matching bra, scented lotion, and a dab of perfume—just under her navel where his nose would be.

"Who?" Jackie sang and giggled to the tap on the dorm room door.

Assuming it was her handsome date delivering some dick, she rushed over and pulled it open. She made a wonder woman-type stance for inspection.

"Damn, shawty!" Pedro practically shouted when he saw her. His eyes ran up and down her curvy black body, recording the sight in his mental. The show got even better when she turned and ran to get her robe. The sight of her booty clapping made him say, "Damn, shawty!" once more. Limited vocabulary, you know.

"Fuck you want!" Jackie demanded, snatching her robe around her. The short, silky garment didn't do much to cover and gave him plenty to gawk at.

"Shit, I came to holla at Meisha, but if she ain't here, we can hang out," he told her thighs. "I ain't heard from shawty in a couple weeks."

It was true since Cameisha refused his calls and ignored his texts after Turbo was killed. She didn't have proof he did it but still didn't trust him. The spell was broken, and she was digusted with herself for fucking with him.

"That's 'cause she don't fuck with you. Take a hint, nigga," she shot back. She had no love for the whole ATL 'shawty-shawty swag' that hooked her roommate.

Jackie shot a glance over the handle of a huge butcher knife that re-placed the gun. She mentally drew a line at his feet and dared him to cross it. The vision of cutting his throat spread a wicked smile on her face. She let go of the robe letting it fall open to lure him in.

Pedro was dumb—no doubt about it—but hood enough to sense the danger. He snapped a few more mental pictures of her crotch as he backed away.

"Tell my bitch I said to call me."

"Bitch? I'll be sure to relay the message, bitch," Jackie dared.

Jackie's date arrived a few minutes after Pedro slinked away. In her frustration, she grudge-fucked him as soon as he walked in. Angry sex is almost as good as make-up sex.

****

"Grandma!" Cameisha screamed as she stepped off the plane. She made a mad dash right into her arms for a tight hug.

After the embrace, Deidra held her at arms-length to inspect her. "Hmp!" She frowned as she looked the girl over.

"Hmp what, Grandma?" Meisha frowned, wondering what was wrong. She showered before she got dressed and knew she didn't stink. She still sniffed her underarms to be sure.

"You got something you need to tell me?" Deidra demanded, frowning deeper.

"I love you? I miss you?" Cameisha asked, still not sure what the woman was talking about. She sniffed again to see if she could detect weed or alcohol on the lady.

"Mm hmp," Grandma repeated, twisting her mouth into the classic, 'yeah right' face.

Deidra let it go and led the girl through the concourse. A hired car awaited on the curb to whisk the women over to the Bronx. Small talk filled the ride to Highbridge.

A brunch of Grandma's braised chicken and her signature carrot raisin salad waited back in the projects. They filled each other in on the events of the last six months as they ate.

"Welp, guess I better get me a nap." Deidra yawned once the table was cleared. She wasn't tired but knew the girl wanted to see her friends but wouldn't have left on her own.

"Okay, guess I'll go check on Sincerity," she said, kissing her granmother's cheek.

Cameisha purposely used the project building's front door. She intended to use the parking lot long way instead of the short cut through the courtyard. It was as cold as December in New York is, and she couldn't stand to see her old friends on that bench. In far too much of a hurry to wait on the pissy elevator, she hopped up the pissy stairs to Sincerity's floor. The smell almost made her lunch come back up.

"Who!" Sincerity barked and snatched her door open. "Chica!"

"Sup, mama? What the hell is that?" Cameisha asked in shock.

"Killa was here!" She laughed, rubbing her protruding belly. "It's a baby. I hope a girl."

"A baby! How you get a baby?" Meisha asked as if she didn't know.

"Your damn uncle!" Sincerity shot back.

"Oh shit! Oh shit!" Cameisha yelled in horror. She took off to the bathroom and upchucked the carrots and raisins.

"You okay? What's wrong, ma?" Sincerity asked from the doorway.

"That's what the hell she was talking about," she replied, thinking of her grandmother's odd behavior. She added her missing period with her reaction to smells and announced, "I'm pregnant!"

"You went all the way to college to get knocked up? You coulda stayed your ass here for that," she said hotly. She was 38 hot at her young friend until the tears came.

"Yo, my grandmother is going to kill me," Meisha sobbed. She totally broke down and wept.

Sincerity came over and wrapped her in her arms. Hugs helped tears flow better, and she let it all out. Cameisha rocked and cried at the thought of fucking up her life. She had a chance and fucked it up.

"Sup with the daddy?" Sincerity asked once the sorrow subsided. "What you gone do?"

"Fuck that bum. I'ma get that bastard's bastard out of me first chance I get!" Cameisha replied. "You got weed?"

"You know I keep a stash for Killa when he come through, hold up," she replied and waddled off to retrieve it.

Only because misery loves company, Cameisha got up and looked out the window. What she saw threatened to start up the tears again. Aqua and Dasia sat huddled together on the park bench they called home. They both frowned from the bitter wind and brutal cold.

"How long have they been there?" she asked when Sincerity returned with the weed.

"How old are they?" She laughed. "Yo, that's their life, ma. Worry about yourself."

"I can't. That's my peeps," Cameisha replied. "Maybe they trappin'!"

"Trappin'? Girl, stop! They fuck for blunts. Everybody done ran through now though," Sincerity shot back.

"I need a couple pounds of green," Meisha announced.

"For what? They just gonna fuck it up."

"Nah, for school and a hammer."

"Pounds of weed and a gun for college? You may as well go have a seat next to them," Sincerity said hotly. "You just like your damn uncle!"

Meisha laughed. "Nah yo, I'm just like my daddy!"

"That nigga E-man over on 164 got some good I hear. Some commercial shit but its straight."

"Same dude who stole my girls' shit and beat them up? I need to holla at him anyway," She growled.

"Check it, ma, that dude is slimy—a killer," Sincerity warned sincerely.

"So am I, make the call!"

Chapter 13

"Say word! Is that who I think it is?" Dasia asked hopefully as Cameisha approached.

Aqua was afraid to look up. How many times had she prayed for their leader to come save them. They were totally lost without guidance and here came their guide. She lifted her head as their savior arrived and lost it.

"Meisha!!" Aqua screamed as she jumped up. She actually tackled Cameisha in the snow and squeezed the air from her lungs.

Dasia jumped on them all and joined the hug. The three girls rolled around in the dirty project snow giggling.

"You back?" Aqua asked hopefully. So many people had left for lofty adventures only to return to the projects. At least they would have memories and stories to tell to those who never made it out.

"Just for Christmans break you. I gotta go back in a couple of weeks," Meisha replied, knocking snow from her coat.

"What happened to you sending for us?" Dasia demanded. All women need leaders, and she wasn't afraid to admit it.

It's fucked up that men—black men—have evolved to just wanting to fuck and leave instead of lead. Somehow pussy became the goal, and once they got it, they were gone. Women have evolved too—evolved to lend themselves and that, too, is fucked up.

"Yo, I had to get settled in yo. I'ma send for y'all," she swore.

"Yesss!" Aqua cheered, bouncing up and down.

"Who at your crib?" Cameisha asked, turning to Dasia.

"Just my moms and dem," she replied even though her mother was alone.

"Bet, let's go up ad smoke this blunt," She offered, showing the weed she got from Sincerity.

It was just like old times as the girls laughed, smoked, and did the Fat-Fat dance. Once the revelry subsided, it was time to get down to business. She cut the music and paused until she had their attention.

"Yo, how y'all fucked up that whole pack?" She demanded.

Both girls made feeble excuses that all led back to them needing to be led. They were worker bees in need of a queen.

"Then E-man took the last of it," Dasia whined with the heartache still evident in her voice.

"A'ight, a'ight," Meisha cut in, cutting off the excuses. "Get dressed to hustle 'cause the Fat-Fat sacks are back! Oh, and y'all gone straighten your face before I leave!"

****

Cameisha squeezed into a pair of super tight jeans and sweater as she dressed for her meeting with E-man. She traded her long leather coat for a short leather jacket to show off her ass. She counted out eight hundred and put it in a purse large enough to hold the weed and set off. A disposable 380 pistol was last into the bag.

"Hmp," Grandma huffed at her backside as she strolled through the living room. "Surprised you can walk in them tight pants."

"Love you too, Grandma." Meisha laughed and blew her a kiss on her way out the door.

Fly girls do not walk, so she hailed a taxi for the two block ride. The cab pulled to a stop in front of the pizza shop on Ogden Avenue. She paid the driver and go out. The pizza shop got quiet instantly as she walked in as if someone hit a mute button. New meat has that effect on men.

"A-yo, ma! I'm ..."

"You aint E-man!" Meisha said, cutting a wannabe playa off.

The youngster rushed her at the door hoping to be first to bag the stranger. Hearing the boss's name sucked all the puffed air from his chest. He lowered his head and pointed to the rear.

"Back here, ma," E-man waved from his booth in the back of the shop. He made sure the back of this hand was seen so she could peep the ice.

"Damn," Meisha said to herself as she approached. Slime ball or no slime ball, the man was fine. The fact that he was obviously getting it only added to it.

The booth cleared of stragglers as she approached. It was empty when she arrived, so she slid in across from E-man.

"My girl told you what I need?" She asked, using her southern charm.

"Yeah, what your pretty ass need with a pound of reefer?" E-man questioned.

"Really, I need more than that. Them kids at my school smoke like a forest fire." she replied. "If this is straight, I'ma need ten mo' fo' I go back to Alabama."

"Yo, it's straight as my dick, ma!" E-man bragged, seeing he had her caught in his charm. Some was real, some was set up, but he was too arrogant to see it.

"I may have to see for myself—both that is," Meisha said seductively. She pulled the roll of money out and placed it on the table.

E-man nodded, and one of his flunkies came and scooped up the money. When he walked out of the pizza shop, Cameisha reached into the bag and clutched the pistol. It would be nice to set him up and beat him like he did her girls, but if no weed appeared soon, she was going to air the pizza shop out.

"It's straight yo," the young hood confirmed when he returned.

He tossed a small brick of compressed weed on the bench next to Meisha. She put it on top of the pistol and stood to leave.

"I'ma hit you for I go back to school," she announced.

"Yeah, and I'ma hit you to before you go," he replied, looking at her crotch. He handed her a card with his number on it as he watched her ass as she walked away.

****

It was just like old times when the girls hit the block with the Fat-Fat. Damn near everybody in the projects smoked weed. In two days time, they had sold completely out and had just over fourteen hundred to show for it. It would have been more if not for smoking and eating.

"You gone get another pack?" Dasia asked. She wondered why Cameisha hadn't split up the money yet.

"Not until it's time to go back to school," She replied.

"I thought you said you were taking us with you?" Aqua said on the verge of hysteria.

"I am, so be ready. But first, y'all gotta handle that business," Meisha demanded.

Cameisha took her friends shopping for the basics before they left. They stocked up on panties, bras, and hygiene items for the trip. Last but not least, they stopped by the sports store in search of payback.

"Damn, that shit is pretty!" E-man exclaimed as he viewed the pussy picture on his phone.

"Thank you." Cameisha giggled even though it wasn't hers. He kept asking for a shot when they spoke, so she got one off the internet. It helped negotiate the price down to 700 per pound for the ten pounds she planned to take south with her.

"A'ight, so check it. I'ma fall through the 'jects with the reefer. We gone fuck and make the deal," he offered.

"Okay." Cameisha giggled girlishly. "Meet me in the lobby of 1440."

"Y'all know what to do, right?" Meisha demanded to her friends when she hung up from the call.

"Yes!" Dasia and Aqua said together.

A few hours later E-man arrived in the projects. He parked in front of the building and grabbed a tote bag from the back seat. Cameisha took a deep breath and prepared for action.

"Hey," she said, switching to country girl mode. It was a good touch for the hard core New Yorker.

"What's good, ma?" he asked, smiling at her short skirt. The big pretty thighs gave him a semi just looking at them.

"My grandma aint left yet, so we can go in the stairwell. I got the money here, and I can suck your dick while we wait," Cameisha offered, sealing the deal.

"Bet!" E-man cheered, now fully erect. He followed her in the stair-case and peeped under her skirt as she led the way up the steps.

"Whew! Here we go," she exclaimed once they reached the top landing of the steps. "Let me get that."

"Hold up, ma, let me see what that head talking about," E-man stalled.

"Okay, let me get that!" she repeated louder this time and looked to the roof door. It was supposed to have burst open, but it didn't. "Let me get that!"

"You ain't gotta beg, baby," he replied and whipped out his dick.

"Let me get that! Let me get that!" Meisha yelled as he approached.

"I think I wanna fuck," E-man decided from the picture of her ass under the skirt.

Cameisha realized she was alone and went for her fun. E-man grabbed her to turn her around just as the gun came out. Seeing it, he went for it as well.

"What, you was gone rob me bitch?" he questioned as he struggled for the gun. He was much bigger and stronger and easily overpowered her. "Let me get it."

The door burst open and in came Aqua and Dasia with bats. Aqua swung, hitting E-man on the arm, causing him to drop the gun. Dasia swung for his head and knocked him to the ground. Cameisha picked up the gun as they beat him.

E-man tried to block the blows with his hands and arms until they were both broken. He covered up as best he could until a blow from

Aqua split his wig and put him to sleep. Meisha fought the urge to shoot him in his head for touching her.

"Grab the weed yo!" she demanded, picking up he bag of money. They had gotten what they came for—revenge. He stole their weed and beat them and they got him back.

"Got it!" Dasia said, grabbing the bag and following her down the steps with Aqua close behind.

"Fuck happened to y'all!" Cameisha asked behind her as they descended the stairs.

"You said to come in when you said, 'Let me get it'; you kept saying, 'Let me get that,'" Aqua replied.

"I told her let's go in," Dasia complained. The two slow girls were arguing while she was fighting off.

"Y'all are fucking cray! Go on to the bus and I'll see y'all tomorrow," Meisha instructed once they hit the lobby.

She had purchased them bus tickets that would get them to Atlanta a few hours after her plane arrived the next day. She wasn't too sure what she was going to do next, but she would not leave them. At least they had the pound of good weed to help figure it out.

The girls went in separate directions once they hit the courtyard. Aqua and Dasia caught a cab to the train to take them to the bus station. Meisha went home to enjoy one last night with Grandma. On the way in she stopped by the trash compactor room to toss away the bag of money, since there was no money in it.

"Are you okay?" Deidra called to Cameisha as she stormed in and rushed down the hall.

"Yes, my period just came on!" she lied over her shoulder.

"Yesss!" Grandma cheered, pumping her fist. She could have sworn the girl was pregnant.

The lie made her take the weed into the bathroom to inspect it. She opened the bag and pulled out a nice brick of compressed weed. Cameisha held the weed to her nose and inhaled deeply.

"Mmm." She smiled at the sweet, pungent aroma. She sat it down and picked up the next one. She inhaled deeply and . . . "Huh?"

The second brick was identical to the first except it had no smell. She tossed it into the tub and pulled out the next and the next. After smelling each of the bricks and getting nothing, she began to open them.

"This nigga here." She laughed at the nine pounds of rabbit food that accompanied the pound of real weed. The thought of him trying to charge her seven grand and some ass for a pound of reefer almost made her go back and shoot him. In the end, she had a pound of free weed and that was a start.

Chapter 14

Cameisha wasn't really sure why she packed the fake weed along with the new clothes she shopped for. Some of the clothes were too big for her which meant she would have to donate them to her roommate, which was the plan anyway. The pound of weed—real and fake—were neatly stacked inside her suitcase.

"And you haven't heard one word I said," Grandma protested as they rode to JFK International Airport.

"Am too! You was telling me how Ms. Jean ain't even go to her grandson's funeral," Cameisha replied, repeating the last words she heard.

Deidra laughed. "Child, that was before we crossed the bridge."

Cameisha cracked a weak smile and then slipped back inside of her head. In there, she had to deal with being pregnant. She had taken three different pregnancy tests, and they all came up positive, and that was negative. Even if she was older and out of school, having a baby by a future inmate or corpse was not a good look. Finding out you had a baby by a deadbeat after the fact sucks, but having a baby by a nigga you know ain't shit is just plain stupid. Meisha was not stupid.

Then there was Aqua and Dasia. What the heck was she going to do with them? One thing for sure is they couldn't stay there after the beating they gave E-man. She had watched an ambulance take him away with regrets. She should have put a bullet in his brain and ended it.

Deidra could only watch her beloved granddaughter wrestle with her problems. It was obvious she had a lot going on and nagging sure wasn't going to help. The woman should teach a class on that. Instead, she reached over and took her hand. Sometimes a good hand hold helps the thought process.

The goodbyes were subdued at the airport. Smiles, hugs, and I love yous eased their departure. Deidra watched with a smile as her college student headed towards her gate. After raising two killers, a college student was a nice change.

Cameisha boarded the plane and found her seat halfway down the plane. Noticing the window seat was vacant, she swapped her aisle seat. Looking out on the tarmac, she went back into her head.

"Excuse me?" a man's voice called out from the aisle.

Cameisha was set to snap on him until she got a look at him.

"What . . . yes?" Cameisha sang delicately at the handsome chocolate man staring down at her.

Disguised as a blink, she ran her eyes up and down his six-foot frame. She decided the clean well-groomed man was worth her attention. Her mind flashed to grimy Pedro and twisted her face into a scowl. The contrast between the dirty thug and this handsome stranger made her shake her head.

"Um, that's my seat but you keep it," he said, confused by her reaction to him.

"Oh, I'm sorry," she apologized profusely and stood.

"No, its fine. I hate sitting by the window," he lied and took her seat. "I'm Bilal."

"Cameisha." Meisha smiled and accepted his strong, outstretched hand and shook it.

"So, you live in Atlanta?" Bilal asked.

"Um, I guess I do. I'm from the Bronx, but I go to Atlanta University."

"Oh cool. That's my alma mata. I just graduated from their medical school," he replied proudly.

"You're a doctor?" Meisha asked eagerly.

"Intern at a clinic but yup, yup. I'm a doctor." He nodded like he couldn't believe it himself.

"That's so cool. I have no idea what I want to do," Cameisha admitted with a frown.

"Sounds like me. I didn't declare a major until halfway through my sophomore year. Drove my parents crazy," he recalled. "When your calling calls, you'll hear it."

Cameisha and Bilal made small talk like a boyfriend/girlfriend interview as the plane sped south. Halfway through the flight, the long night came back and put her to sleep. The jolt of the plane landing in Atlanta finally roused her from her sleep. She found herself resting peacefully on his shoulder.

"My bad," she said, embarrassed as she wiped her slobber from his shirt.

"No problem." He laughed. "Can we . . . um . . . you know . . . um . . . exchange numbers?" he asked shyly.

"Sure!" Cameisha cheered. His shyness was a refreshing change. All the guys in school were so rude and aggressive. Even Pedro would call and ask, "Can I fuck?"

The thought of his crude manners and crass behavior caused her to frown again. Even though the sex was great, he charged her for her dignity; in exchange was 'suck my dick' every day, but that wasn't happening.

The conversation continued through the airport all the way to baggage claim. Luckily for Meisha, Bilal only had a carry-on bag, so they said their goodbyes. She would have been too embarrassed to get caught with weed in front of doctor hunk.

Cameisha drug the large suitcase to the train and headed back to school. From the train, she hopped a taxi back to the dorm.

"Meisha!" Jackie cheered when her buddy walked into the room. She jumped up and ran over to hug her at the door.

"I missed you, too." Cameisha laughed as Jackie lifted her off her feet in a tight embrace. "So what I miss?"

"Well for one, I've been getting my boots knocked really, really well." She laughed honestly. Her grad student boyfriend had practically moved into her vagina. "Yo' girl, Cynthia, stopped by every five minutes looking for weed. Oh and your dumb ass boyfriend came by. Told the nigga you wasn't here and he tried to holla at me."

"He a bum alright. His bum ass done knocked me up too," she fumed.

"I'm sorry, what did you say?" Jackie asked ever so politely. She cocked her ear to the side so she could hear better.

"I'm pregnant," she repeated. "Can't believe I let that nigga knock me up."

Jackie nodded then popped her right in her mouth. "That's what I thought you said."

"Fuck you do that for?" Meisha demanded through bloody lips.

"Put your hands up yo. I need one!"

"Girl, I ain't finna fight you," she said, looking at her blood on her fingers.

That was the wrong answer, and Jackie popped her again. Again, she protested and got popped. By the fourth straight jab to her mouth, Cameisha finally fought back. She howled and rushed in. Meisha went low and scooped Jackie off her feet.

"Ugh!"

They both went down with a thud and wrestled for supremacy. The girls were rolling around trying to pin each other when the door flew open.

"Y'all got weed?" Cynthia questioned down at then, ignoring the fight.

"Actually . . . let me get up, girl," Cameisha replied and stopped fighting. Jackie stopped too, and they both stood. "I do but you gotta come back."

"How long?" Cynthia asked, looking at her watch. She intended to hold her to whatever she said to the second.

"Give me like an hour to get unpacked," she replied. As soon as Cynthia set her watch, she walked out.

Meisha turned to her friend. "A-yo, what was all that about?" she demanded.

"'Cause I'd rather kill you then see you throw your life away over some bum! That's the type of niggas we left behing in New York; why the fuck you slumming? And you ain't having that baby!"

"I already know. I need to hurry up and take care of it 'cause I met a doctor." She smiled with bloody lips.

As they spoke, she opened her bag and started unloading.

"Yo, you came on the plane with that!" Jackie exclaimed when the weed came into view.

"Only one is real. Nigga tried to flex me so me and my girls got on that ass! Oh! That reminds me . . ."

****

"There they go!" Cameisha cheered as Aqua and Dasia stepped off the bus. They both squinted in the bright sunshine as they got their first view of Atlanta.

It was their first trip outside of New York City. In fact, the girls—like a lot of New Yorkers—rarely left their home borough. Besides the occasional foray over into Manhattan, they were BX for life.

When they spotted Cameisha running towards them, they took off to meet her halfway. The trio slammed into each other as if they hadn't just left each other the day before.

"Jackie, these my girls, Aqua and Dasia," Meisha introduced.

"Hey," Jackie, Aqua, and Dasia all said stoically. They all had that look of smelling a foul odor as that new friend/old friend jealousy/rivalry entered their lives.

The girls didn't have many bags since they didn't own much stuff. They grabbed their meager possessions and boarded the Marta train adjacent the bus station.

Jackie regretted her decision to let the girls stay with them the second they walked into the dorm room. The space was right for two, but two more was too much.

"This my bed!" Aqua shouted and dived on Jackie's freshly made bed. Jackie bit her tongue and turned to Cameisha.

"Y'all chicks on the floor," Meisha demanded playfully. "Now help me bag up."

Jackie pouted as the three teens reminisced about life in their projects. They spread newspaper on the rug and bagged up the pound into tiny bite-sized dime bags. She wanted no parts of being a drug dealer, so she didn't help.

Cynthia was spreading the word so quickly that fifty of the two hundred dimes sold in hours. Aqua and Dasia handled sales while Cameisha and Jackie attended classes. In two days, all the weed was gone, and she had to figure out how to get more.

But first, she had a more pressing problem to worry about.

Chapter 15

"Man, this some bullshit," Cameisha complained as she boarded the train to downtown.

When she reached her stop, she got off and followed directions to her destination. After checking the address on her paper against the sign on the building, she pulled the handle but found it locked.

"This is some bullshit!" she repeated and pressed the buzzer.

"How can I help you?" a woman's voice asked through the intercom.

Cameisha cocked her head curiously and frowned at the question. Was she really expected to announce, 'I'm here for an abortion'? She flirted with the idea of turning around and walking away, but the consequences of that far outweighed the momentary embarrassment . . . or so she thought.

She leaned in and spoke into the intercom. "I got an appoint yo."

"Name?" the woman asked.

"Forrest, Cameisha Forrest," she replied, wishing she had used an alias. She should have said her name was Shayla or Imanni or Athea.

A full minute passed before the door clicked loudly from being remotely unlocked. She stepped inside only to find another locked door. It wasn't until the first one was completely closed that the second was unlocked.

"I.D., please," an armed security guard asked when she stepped fully inside.

Cameisha complied and produced her school I.D. She didn't understand the frown on his face as he inspected it. It troubled him how many young girls from the local colleges ended up in here. It made him think about the teen he had at home preparing for college next year.

"Go on and have a seat," the guard said, stopping just short of adding 'with the rest', referring to the three other college girls waiting to terminate the results of poor choices and wreckless sex.

Cameisha grabbed a book from the table and took a seat in the cold waiting room. It was kept near freezing so the cold examination rooms wouldn't shock them.

"Man, this some bullshit," Meisha groaned as a glance up at the clock revealed two hours had passed. Luckily, she was reading Dungeon Master by Yara Kaleemah, and the time passed quickly. She was all into reading about Nick when she heard her name.

"Cameisha Forrest?" a nurse called as she read the name from a chart without looking up. She very rarely made eye contact or looked in the women's faces. That was way too personal for the woman working in the wrong job. Killing babies as a form of birth control was too much for her.

Cameisha rasied her hand but didn't call our 'here' as she stood. When she made it over to the nurse, the woman turned on her heels and led her into the back.

Meisha looked at her colorful scrubs and matching sneakers and smiled. The thought of being a nurse crossed her mind but didn't stop. It was dismissed with a shake of the head, but the smile remained as thoughts of her doctor friend popped into her head.

She and Bilal had been trading text messages since they got back to Atlanta. He kept asking her out, but she stalled him. Once she got the bastard baby out of her belly, she would give him her full attention and anything else he wanted.

"In here," the nurse said, opening the door to an examination room.

Once inside, the woman took vital signs, blood, and asked a series of questions designed to gleam sexual and medical history. The forty-something nurse was shocked at how much the college girls were fucking. Most reported multiple partners and no protection.

"Put this on, hop on the table with your feet up, and the doctor will see you shortly," she said, handing her a flimsy gown.

"Man, this some bullshit," Meisha mumbled as she complied.

The clinic was set up like a vaginal assembly line. The nurses would prep the woman so the doctor could come in and get to work. All tests done, feet in stirrups, no faces, just vaginas.

"Let's see what we got here," the doctor announced with a sigh as he stepped in, causing Cameisha to frown at the familiar voice.

The doctor's sigh was genuine because in his short tenure at the clinic he had seen some really beat up boxes. Some were layed open like a baked potato, while others looked like somebody played soccer with it. At least one a day came in full of cum, but not this one. This neatly-shaved, clean vagina threatened to give him a rather unprofessional erection.

"Test shows you're definitely pregnant, so we will perform the procedure," he said, speaking into her vagina. The voice was so familiar she had to look down and make sure it wasn't.

"Man, this some bullshit!" Cameisha groaned, seeing Bilal between her legs.

"Cameisha!" he screamed in fear. He had been dying to see the girl from the plane again, but not like this. "I . . . um . . . I . . . I'll get a colleague," Bilal stammered and ran from the room.

A few moments later, a white lady doctor came to complete the procedure. Cameisha couldn't help but cry as she was poked, prodded, and relieved of the unwanted pregnancy.

"Take this," the doctor said, handing her a pill. "You will be sore since you obviously haven't had much sex. So take one every four hours but do not abuse them!"

"Yes ma'am," Cameisha said, popping her first Oxy.

Not having a ride meant she had to wait in the waiting room for a few hours before being allowed to leave. She picked Dungeon Master back up and continued where she left off. The pill kicked in, and not only was the pain gone but she was as happy as she had ever been in her life. The pill had her high as a kite.

"Need a ride?" Bilal asked, coming upon her. "Come on," he answered for her and led her to his car.

The ride to the college was quiet except for the radio playing. They both wanted to speak but no words came out of their mouths. He wanted an excuse or explanation as bad as she wanted to give one. When Bilal stopped at the dorm, he finally spoke up.

"Guess I'll see you around," he offered but made it sound like a question.

"I guess," she replied and ran into the building so he wouldn't see her cry.

Chapter 16

"I sure hope you know what you're doing?" Cameisha asked as the train doors began to close. The question was to herself, but she still pondered before answering.

She looked over at her friends standing in the door watching Atlanta pass by as they pointed and cheered. She had an obligation to them and knew they were counting on her. The week they spent in the tight dorm room was too much. She had to get them a place. That meant she needed more money, which meant she needed more weed.

After trying and failing to find some good weed at a good price, she decided to act. Taking a chapter from her Dope Boy father's book, she was in search of a Mexican connect. She was headed across town to where all the Latino people congregated. Buford Highway had a huge Spanish, as well as Asian, population. This is where she would start her search.

The two thousand dollars in cash sat on top of a pistol in her purse. The small 380 only held six shots, but she knew if push came to shove, both Aqua and Dasia would push and shove.

A good connect was needed for the girls to maintain themselves. Cameisha's money wouldn't last no time trying to pay rent and feed them. When the train pulled to a stop at the Chamblee Station, they got out and found a taxi. A short ride later, she spotted their destination.

"Right there, pull in there!" Cameisha instructed.

The driver complied and pulled into the parking lot of the Buford Highway Flea Market.

"Looks like we in Mexico!" Dasia exclaimed, seeing the throngs of Latinos.

Although largely Mexican, the droves of people came from every country in Central and South America you could think of. There were

Hondurans, Costa Ricans, as well as a few Colombians. Music blared from at least three different sources, and the air was a mix of aromas.

"Smells like we in the right place," Meisha announced, smelling all the weed in the air.

"Sure do!" Aqua cheered, smelling her favorite dish—Arroz Con Pollo—which translates to chicken and rice.

"First things first," Cameisha said, missing the dish herself.

She scanned the faces and attire of all the men as they strolled through the parking lot. The older men dressed like cowboys in Buddy Lee jeans and cowboy hats with big ass belt buckles got dismissed. So did the young ones blasting rap music and dressed like black kids. Carefully, she scrutinized . . . until she saw him.

The handsome young man walked with the gait of royalty. He was tastefully dressed with select pieces of jewelry that indicated he was getting it. The bad chick on his arm had gold digger written all over her, so no way he was a broke nigger.

"Wait here," Meisha told her friends and made a bee line to the man.

He didn't look like the type of dude you ran up on, so she went alone. He looked curious as she approached while the woman scrunched her pretty face up.

"Quien tiene yierba?" She asked, getting straight to the point.

"Yierba?" he asked as if he didn't understand the word then pointed over to a group of young guys passing a blunt around. "Ask them," he said in perfect English.

"I'm not tryna cop a dime sack. I need a few pounds," Cameisha said, staring into his pupils. The eyes can't lie, and his said he could get it.

"Few pound huh?" he said, scanning her from head to toe. Her expensive yet subdued clothes told him she was official. Niggas in turned up shoes or dirty pants don't buy weight.

Cameisha was dressed comfortably in a pink sweatsuit by ONE UMMAH, pink Tims, and pink leather jacket. She passed the test.

"I'm sure my friend should have a couple of pounds to sell," he said casually. His companion frowned slightly and shot him a glance that told on him. He was the friend he spoke of. "You have a number?"

"Sure do," She replied, going into her pink backpack for her pen and *My Little Pony* notepad. "What's the ticket?"

"For you . . ." he paused, earning another frown from his woman. In an instant, Cameisha's mind visioned beating her up like she did Arnell. "Give me six each."

"Bet!" Cameisha shouted then caught herself and regained her cool. "I'll take three."

"Okay, Ca . . . mee . . . sha," he said, reading her name from the paper. "I'm Juan. I will call you later."

Cameisha nodded her approval as he led his woman away. She was chewing him out real good in rapid fire Spanish. Since she was fluent in the language, she knew she was the subject of the beef.

"I don't know why bitches think I want their man," she questioned, watching Juan's ass while he walked away.

"What's up?" Aqua and Dasia asked hopefully when Cameisha walked back over.

"We bout to come up is what's up!" she shot back.

"Now for some Arroz Con Pollo!"

****

"Hola, chica," Juan said when Cameisha answered his call. She had hoped the unknown number was his and smiled upon hearing his voice. His tone also said his woman wasn't around.

"Who's calling?" Cameisha asked coyly as she stifled a giggle.

"Yeah right." Juan laughed.

He was slightly flirtatious, using adjectives like sweetheart, as they arranged the sale of three pounds of Mexican marijuana. The Colombian actually had a ton of the stuff. He never handled sales himself but made an exception for her. Something about the cute kid got to him, but it wasn't sexual. Oddly, he felt a big brother/little sister affection to the stranger.

As soon as she hung up, Cameisha popped an Oxy and washed it down with her soda. The three girls in the room all frowned when they saw her. Jackie was the only one who knew about the abortion, but they all were concerned about the pills.

"You still in pain?" Jackie asked, arching an eyebrow as a question mark.

She knew all too well that people abused pain pills. That was some girls' hustle when she was in prison. They would fake injury to go to medical then sell the pills. Cynthia had been offering her twenty-five dollars, but Cameisha, the hustler, turned her down and took them herself. That worried Jackie.

"Chill, ma, I got this." Cameisha giggled. She was still high from the last pill and giddy from the conversation with Juan.

An hour later, Juan texted from downstairs, announcing his arrival. She quickly recounted eighteen one hundred dollar bills and grabbed a small tote bag. She wasn't sure what type of car he drove, so she glanced around once she stepped outside. She would have seen Pedro parked from his stalking position had Juan not flashed his lights at her. Pedro growled as he watched her hips sway seductively as she rushed to get into the customized Sedan. The handsome goon didn't take rejection well. He wanted to get her back so he could dump her. It was all about control.

"Oh!" Cameisha exclaimed when the Lambo door swung upward. She slid in, and Juan hit the button that let it back down. "Hey, Juan," she sang in the singsong tone girls use when they like a boy. She liked this boy.

"Hold, bonita, coma esta?" he said, flashing that bright smile that went so well with the golden skin and dark eyes.

Confusing affinity as affection, she had to fight the urge not to lean in and kiss him. Instead, she replied, "Muy bien gracious, y tu?"

"I'm good, mamacita. I have your stuff," he said and reached into the back seat. He produced a large Ziploc bag stuffed with what looked like fluffy green popcorn. The pungent smell coming through the plastic bragged on its quality.

"Looks good." She nodded casually, but the look on her face said, 'Oh shit, this some good shit!'

The dope girl weighed it by sight and feel and confirmed it was three pounds at least. In fact, it was several ounces over. She handed over the cash, and he popped open the center console and tossed it in without counting. In the few seconds the compartment was open, Cameisha spied another bundle of cash and a plastic pistol—a glock, her favorite. She wanted to ask if he could get one for her but decided to wait.

"So, where's your girl? She let you come out without her?" Cameisha heard herself ask. She was mad at her mouth for speaking without permission, but since it was in the air, she waited for a reply.

"My fiancé is very jealous even though she doesn't need to be. She is number one," Juan replied.

"Well, I ain't nobody's side piece!" her mouth spat again. She thought about covering the hole with her hand before it said anything crazy.

"My friend has this on a regular, so let me know when you are ready," Juan said, letting her statement pass.

"Can you get Oxys? I need . . . um, they sell good too," she requested.

"Unfortunately, I have yet to find a good source. We have coke, weed, and meth but no Oxy. Not yet anyway," he said, revealing himself.

"A-yo, what's the ticket if I buy weight?" Meisha asked, thinking like a dope girl should.

"You mean like a hundred pounds? I can go—"

"No! I meant like ten or so!" Meisha cut in.

"For you, five a piece," he said. "Call when you are ready."

"Will do, papi," Meisha said and got out.

Pedro followed her with his eyes as she rushed back into the building. He meant to follow Juan too, but he was gone by the time his eyes unglued from Cameisha's ass. He was in such a foul mood, he went to one of his baby mama's house and took it out on her. First, he beat the pussy up, and then her to make himself feel better.

Chapter 18

"This shit is that shit!" Cynthia cheered at the sight of the new weed. She was unofficially a sales person too since she knew all the other pot-heads and druggies.

Being a middle man, she earned a little money or weed as she shuttled all over campus. This allowed her to spend her generous allowance on the high-end clothes she loved almost as much as getting high.

"Still ain't coming off none of them Oxys?" Cynthia asked greedily.

"No!" Cameisha snapped, startling everyone in the room.

Aqua and Dasia were bagging up tiny dimes to squeeze every dime out of the package. They were eager to get some money up so they could get away from Jackie, who had enough of company. She would say little things to let them know they had worn out their welcome. Stuff like, "Y'all worn out your welcome."

Luckily for all, the first pound of potent weed sold in a day. The nearly two thoussand dollars in small bills looked like a million dollars to the girls, especially Jackie. She wanted no parts of the operation but still felt left out. Cameisha still looked out for her, but it wasn't like having your own.

"Time to get an apartment!" Meisha announced when she counted out 1,800 dollars.

"Yes!!!" Aqua cheered and broke out doing the Fat-Fat dance.

The Fat-Fat dance was contagious, so Meisha and Dasia got up and joined her. Jackie turned her lips at the display. Prison caused her to miss this age of life, and it stung. Slowly, a smile spread on her face, and she stood too.

"Y'all show me this damn dance!" she demanded.

****

A nearby apartment complex catered to the college student. Cameisha's school I.D. got them a hundred dollar move-in special. The six hundred dollar deposit was the same amount as the monthly rent, but the first month's rent was reduced to a hundred bucks.

"Ohh, this my room!" Dasia sang as they ran around the vacant unit for the first time.

It had two bedrooms, and she had selected the large master bedroom with bathroom as her own. The other bedroom was about the same size as the dorm room they all currently shared. Actually, Cameisha had planned to keep that one herself.

"Ooh, that's y'all room," she said, changing her mind and alerting them to the fact that they would be sharing a room.

"Okay," they said in unison like they often did. They were so used to sharing a project bedroom with siblings, cousins, and aunts; two to a room was luxury. Plus, it was their own.

There was still about 1,200 dollars left after paying for the apartment. Two hundred went to get the lights and cable turned on which left a stack to spend at Walmart.

The deal was to hold back re-coup plus fifty percent of sales. That meant that out of the two grand they stood to make off a pound, nine hundred went to the cause while they split the rest three ways. That meant over three hundred dollars a piece. The first pound sold in a day, so at that rate, they stood to make over two grand a week.

The crew each pushed a shopping cart through the local Walmart, filling it with household items. Air mattresses served as bedroom sets for now. They bought pots and pans, plants, and flatware. Cute bath sets were picked for both bathrooms and, of course, a TV and stereo to put in front of the two futons they purchased for the living room.

It took two taxis to get all the stuff back to the apartment, but the girls weren't done yet. After setting their haul inside, they hit the supermarket to load up on junk food and frozen meals.

The next pound sold in a little more than a day, so a little shopping was in order. Since Cynthia had a car, she drove, and Jackie tagged along, armed with her stipend check. The whole twenty five dollars.

"I'll meet you guys in the food court," Cynthia blurted and was a blur as she took off to the mall's high-end store.

"Holla!" Aqua echoed and made a beeline to a plus-sized store named Big Girls Need Luv.

"I'ma see what they talking about up in here," Dasia said, slinking off towards the low-end boutique. The gaudy outfits in the window said the store sold all the gear a hoochie mama would need for a club night.

"Guess it's you and me," Cameisha said as she and Jackie strolled through the mall.

The conversation was light and friendly, but Meisha knew something was on her friend's mind. She also knew her well enough to let her bring it out on her own.

Jackie watched as Cameisha selected mid-thigh teal-colored suede shorts and suede knee-length boots; a blouse a shade lighter completed the ensemble. While she tried it on, Jackie searched the racks for something her twenty-five bucks could purchase and found nothing.

"Does my ass look fat in this?" Cameisha asked. She came fully out of the dressing room and turned around to show her ass like a facebook picture.

"Yes," Jackie answered honestly. Truth be told, the girl had a fat ass, so everything made her look like she had a fat ass.

"Good!" Meisha cheered since that's what she was going for. She rushed back into the dressing room to change back into her clothes.

"You ain't find nothing?" she asked as they reached the checkout counter and saw her friend was empty-handed.

"No, I, um . . . a-yo, put me down," Jackie said, making up her mind.

"Down with what?" she asked although she knew the answer. She had to ask to get put on; there would be no more handouts. Not with her and the girls grinding to get it.

"I want in with you, Dasia, and Aqua. I wanna help. I wanna shop too," she admitted.

"'Bout time. You can hold down the fort while we go party!" Cameisha exclaimed.

The girls met at the food court and shared meals from six different restaurants. After filling their bellies, they headed home to shower and change because it was party time!

Chapter 19

"Oh hell to the naw!" Cynthia protested at the sign for twenty dollar valet parking. Cameisha woulda sprung for it, but she already pulled off.

They parked a few blocks away on Peachtree Street in a free lot and walked back to the club. Just as they arrived at the trendy club, a Benz full of fly girls came to a giggling stop. Four bad bitches in a bad ass Porsche hopped out and paid the valet. The doorman lifted the velvet rope and got a tip as they giggled past him. Meisha suddenly felt plain and didn't like it. She was a bad bitch, too, and saw her future.

She felt mixed emotions an hour ago when she swallowed the last of the pills that made her soar. It had kicked in, and she felt great, but what about tomorrow?

"Erv-G!" Dasia screamed when they walked in and saw her favorite rapper on the stage. He was shirtless and sweaty as he ran through a medley of his hits. Dasia rushed towards the stage, pushing girls out of her way as she went.

"Groupie!" Meisha called at her back, but it was wasted. "Come on, y'all."

She looked at the entrance of the V.I.P. section and sighed. That was where she belonged, but it was beyond her reach—at the moment anyway. They settled for a table that offered a good view of the crowded dance floor and V.I.P. She couldn't help but notice that most of the chics up there were groupies. Sipping champagne and smoking weed on ass credit. The dope boys and rappers were putting the pussy on layaway until after the after-party. Some had hands under short skirts playing in the coochie while they partied. Cameisha knew she belonged up there but not as a groupie. No, she was meant to pop bottles.

"Say, shawty, ain't that yo' girl over there?" Big Shawty said when he spotted Cameisha and company at their table. He loved the fact that she dumped him and threw it in his face every chance he got. Shawty fought off a smile, watching his jaw tighten when he saw her.

"Bitch swear she all that," Pedro growled jealously.

They sipped on cheap beer while the girls guzzled glasses of colorful cocktails. Guys flocked and swarmed around the table full of pretty girls.

When Cynthia got up to use the bathroom, Pedro came up with a plan. In his little mind, fucking one of her friends would be get back, so that's what he set out to do. While she was inside peeing, he was waiting outside plotting.

"Sup, Miss Molly?" Pedro said, and then flashed his golds.

Just like fat kids love cake, Cynthia loved drugs. The mention of pure MDMA known as mollies could not be passed up. Cameisha only had weed and wouldn't sell or share any of her Oxy.

"You got some?" the future addict asked intently.

"We can go cop some if you wanna hang out. You wanna hang out?" Pedro asked, pouring on the charm.

"Sure! Let me go tell my girls I'm leaving," Cynthia said. She turned around then stopped in her tracks. She wasn't hardly 'bout to leave a club with a strange guy to get high and have sex and didn't know his name. So she asked, "What's your name?"

"Call me . . . um . . . Dre," he replied. It was close to his real name, but his brain didn't respond quickly. Had he had more time, he could have come up with something better.

"Okay, I'm Cynthia," she said. Having exchanged names took being a hoe out of the equation.

"We can run a train on that hoe!" Big Shawty announced eagerly. Most of the pussy he got was scraps and leftovers, so he hoped his partner would put him down.

"You gone hafta get you a junky tonight, Shawty. This one is special," Pedro said, plotting. This girl was his way to get in Cameisha's business, not to mention she was fine.

"Where's Aqua at?" Cynthia asked with a curious frown when she returned to find Meisha alone at the table.

For a reply, she pointed over to the dance floor. There was Aqua working it out with a football player. They were battling step for step, dance move for dance move. It was a tie until Erv-G went into his Fat-Fat song. Being one of the originators, she ate him up and got a round of applause from the dance floor.

"I'm 'bout to go. Me and my friend. . . um . . . Dave?" Cynthia frowned, trying to remember his name. She almost said Molly since that was where her mind was. The pure MDMA beat the hell out of the generic ecstasy tabs polluted with God knows what.

"Bye, hoe," Cameisha teased, but Cynthia left so fast she missed it.

"Erv-G want me to come to the hotel with him!" Dasia cheered, bouncing up and down and clapping her hands like she hit the Powerball. She turned and took off before Meisha could respond.

Next was Aqua. Cameisha watched her approach the table holding a linebackers hand. She let go a few feet from the table and came alone.

"I um . . ."

"Met a guy?" Cameisha asked, helping her along.

"Yes!" She giggled.

"And you 'bout to go home with him?" Meisha added.

"Yes." Aqua giggled shyly.

"Use protection and have fun," she advised.

"I can't get pregnant anyway," Aqua reminded since her mother had her fixed years ago.

"No, but you can get burned, clap, AIDS," Cameisha shot back.

Aqua smiled, nodded, and took off.

Cameisha finished her drink through a swarm of come ons and stood to leave. She stepped from the club and pulled her phone from her purse to call for a taxi. A glance at the screen showed several missed calls and two voicemails. After calling for a taxi, she checked the messages. The first was from Jackie.

"A-yo, this shit is crazy yo! People been coming like every few seconds for these shits. I sold about fifty of them already!" she yelled into the phone.

Cameisha heard what she didn't say—that she was hooked. Money is far more addictive than any drug. That's because you can do so much more with it. The dealers are the real junkies.

The next call was from an unknown number that would have been sent to voicemail anyway. She hit the button and listened to see who and what it was about.

"Hey . . . um, Cameisha, this is . . . um, Bilal. I . . . um, I'm saying, I . . . look, I cannot ignore our connection. I don't know what's going on in your life but I . . . well, this is my new number, so you can call me," Bilal managed to get out.

"Okaay!" Meisha giggled then listened to the message again.

The cab pulled up in the middle of the third playback and dropped her off at the apartment by the tenth.

****

That night was the first time Jackie directly sold drugs, but it was a night of firsts for all of the girls. It was the first time Cameisha had been to an adult club and as for the rest of the girls . . .

"Be right back, shawty," Pedro announced as he pulled to a stop in front of a house in Midtown.

He ran inside and copped a few grams of powdered molly from a white dealer he dealt with. In a flash, he was back in the car headed for the hood. Knowing there were too many people at the trap house, he decided to spring for a hotel—well, motel actually. Pedro was a cheap nigga to his core, but this was an investment, so he parted ways with thirty bucks for two hours. The clock began when he took the keys, so he had to work fast.

The pampered rich girl frowned as she walked into the dank motel room behind Pedro. She was use to four or five-star hotels, but this place smelled like a pamper.

"Oh!" she exclaimed as the smell hit her nose. She realized it was futile to try to hold her breath, so she took sips of air to stay alive.

Pedro went over to the small table and emptied the package of powder on the table. Using his expired driver's license, he made three lines on the table. He rolled a bill into a straw and snorted one line in half then switched nostrils and inhaled the rest.

"Here," he offered, passing the bill to Cynthia.

She accepted it quickly and snorted both lines even quicker. In an instant, electric currents ran through her being.

"Drank?" Pedro asked, pouring a generous shot of liquor into a paper cup and a splash of soda.

"Umm . . . sure," She replied curiously at his past tense use of the word as well as the off-brand products. The can of soda actually said, 'drank' and listed the flavor as blue. "I would love some drank."

He tossed his drank back, and she followed suit. Since they were playing follow the leader, Pedro stood and stripped. The clock was ticking, so he had to move on to the main event.

The drugs had Cynthia needing to be touched. She quickly peeled off her designers to get naked. She scanned his muscular build and settled her eyes on his rock hard erection. His nuts had a musty odor, but she was past the point of return.

They met in the middle of the sex-stained bed. Pedro roughly snatched her leg in the air by an ankle and plunged inside of her. The roughneck thug fucked the daylights out of the prissy dive. She changed her mind about it being a one-night stand. He could get it anytime he wanted.

Pedro grunted and came inside of her. She had meant to tell him to pull out, but that would have fucked up her own orgasm. Her mind flashed to her supply of Morning-after pills that she kept for accidents such as this.

"You do coke?" Pedro asked before pulling out of her.

"Sure! You got some?" she replied eagerly.

There weren't too many drugs Cynthia didn't do. If you had it, she would give it a try. He picked his dingy jeans up and produced another small package. Cynthia followed him over to the table where he made a few more lines, only this time he didn't do one. One of the side effects of coke is a limp noodle. He needed his dick so he passed.

"So, who got the weed at your school now?" he asked casually as she snorted the coke.

Cocaine is the truth serum, and she began to tell all she knew about Cameisha's operation. Since she was an unofficial member of the crew, she knew all about Cameisha's operation.

Pedro was a hater deep in his heart anyway, but hearing how much better she was doing than him had him steamed. She wasn't even from his city, and she already had a connect. He may not be much of a dope boy, but at least he had another occupation to fall back on—armed robbery.

****

Dasia did indeed get invited back to the hotel, but she was one of many. Rapper Erv-G was a big freak and needed some freaks to freak with. Once they arrived at the five-star hotel, a bodyguard spread the refreshments on the table.

When the groupies all bent over to snort coke off the table, Dasia followed suit. All the girls smoked, snorted, and sipped with the rapper's entourage. Only a few would be invited back into the bedroom to have the honor of fucking the superstar. The rest would gladly settle for the DJ, security, hype man, and homeboys. At least they could still brag that they went back to Erv-G's hotel room and got fucked. They would leave out the part of it being his barber or driver of course.

"You, you, and . . .you," Erv-G said as he selected his bedmates for the night.

Dasia was picked second and actually clapped.

Inside the inner sanctum, the rapper had them all strip and dance while he captured it on his phone as he smoked a blunt.

"Y'all kiss," he instructed, and they all said, "Okay."

Dasia complied too.

It was Dasia's first time kissing a girl, and she liked it. A few minutes into the make-out session one of the girls ate her pussy—also a first. She liked that too. Liked it so much she returned the favor and that, too, she liked. The girls made each other cum several times while snorting coke in-between.

"Y'all give me some head," the rapper ordered, and they rushed to comply. They fought playfully over his manhood then took turns pleasing him.

After fucking the three girls in every known position, Erv-G dismissed them. A bodyguard loaded them in one of the cars and dropped them off around Atlanta.

"Lisa," one of the girls said as the car pulled in front of her house. She pushed her number into his hand and got out.

Dasia tried coke and pussy for the first time that night, but it would not be the last. She got out at the apartment with hunger and thirst.

****

Aqua and her new friend spent the rest of the night rearranging the furniture in his dorm room. The large couple fucked on the small bed until dawn. Being the southern gentleman that he was, he fed her waffles before dropping her off at the apartment.

Chapter 20

Cameisha and Bilal traded text messages and frequent phone calls for weeks. Their affection grew by the day. Finally, the day came when she agreed to go out with him. He took her to a swank little Indian restaurant in hopes of impressing her. He succeeded.

"This is nice!" Meisha exclaimed as he led her by the hand into the dimly lit establishment.

"It is. I'm glad you like it," he replied proudly. He often took dates here because of the ambiance and five known aphrodisiacs on the menu.

The tables sat low to the ground, requiring patrons to sit on large fluffy pillows. Most of the fare was meant to be eaten by hand, so that's how they ate.

"Try this one," Bilal offered, pusing a piece of spicy chicken towards her face. Cameisha allowed him to put it in her mouth with a giggle.

By the second course, the hand feeding had become seductive. Intense eye contact now accompanied the savory shrimp they put in each other's mouths. When Cameisha closed her mouth around his finger and slowly sucked it, it was time to go.

"Check, please!" Bilal yelled so loud he startled the couple dining next to them.

The desert menu had been changed, so Bilal sped back to his condo. The ride was quiet because the air was filled with a sexual current that didn't require words. She absorbed the soft jazz and was comfortable with her decision to let him have her.

"Would you like the tour?" he asked as they entered his tidy unit.

Cameisha cracked a sly smile and shook her head no.

When they reached the bedroom, the future lovers stood on opposite sides of the platform bed and slowly stripped shirt for shirt, then wife beater for bra, his slacks followed by her jeans, boxer briefs and panties, until they were both naked.

The couple crawled towards each other on the bed and met with a kiss in the middle. They maintained lip contact as they lay down. Meisha resisted the urge to touch him with her hands, but Bilal didn't. As their tongues got acquainted, he reached down between her legs. As he fondled her neatly-shaved box, he played in its slippery wetness.

He kissed his way to her neck then breasts. By the time he got one of her hard nipples in his mouth, she moaned from an orgasm. Bilal made sure each plump titty got equal treatment as he kissed, sucked, and caressed them.

"Mmm," Cameisha whined when the kisses moved down to her hard stomach.

He moved lower and pushed her thighs apart, kissing and sucking them well. Cameisha almost protested when he put his face between her legs. One flick of his tongue on her non-swollen clit was enough to shut her up.

Meisha's back arched, and she hissed loudly as he massaged her pussy with his lips and tongue. He had to hold her down by placing a hand on her stomach to prevent her from levitating. She came again more violently than the first and soaked his face with her fluids.

Bilal quickly kissed his way back and put his tongue in her mouth. Cameisha could taste her own sweetness as he reached for a condom from a bowl of assorted variety on the nightstand. He tore it open with his teeth and rolled it down on his erection.

"Put it in!" Cameisha demanded. She was desperate to have him inside of her immediately.

"No, you do it," he ordered, staring down at her.

She complied by grabbing his stiff manhood. It wasn't quite as thick as Pedro's but just as long. She worked the head in the fluid leaking out of her then positioned it between her lips. When he wouldn't push, she grabbed him by the hips and pulled him inside of her.

Bilal slow-stroked her to a quick orgasm while maintaining eye contact the whole time. He treated her to another then picked up the pace as his own drew near. Cameisha heard herself cheer. She was embarrassed by the outburst, but some emotions go straight from the heart to the mouth without stopping by the brain.

"Mine, too," Bilal replied, scanning his memories to see if it was true. He nodded affirmatively content that if not the best, it was certainly up there.

Cameisha watched as he carefully removed the condom. She twisted her lips thinking how much drama that small piece of latex could have saved her from.

"Incoming mail," the laptop on the desk announced as the couple cuddled.

"And it can wait!" Bilal shouted playfully back to the computer. "Probably one of these pill mills wanting more Oxy for their legal junkies!"

"Oxy!" Cameisha shouted and bolted upright in the bed. "I mean, what's a pill mill?"

It had been a couple of weeks since she last swallowed one of the pills that made her feel so good. She had been trying to make up for the loss by smoking blunts with her friends. That really wasn't working because for one it was too much work. You had to roll the weed, smoke the weed, pass the weed, use Visine for your eyes, mints for your breath, and perfume to hide the smell. Not Oxy though, just pop and take off. It was a high she could function with.

"So-called pain management clinics. Really just a way for white people to sell dope and not go to prison," he fumed. "They order bulk supplies at discount rates, and then dispense at full street value to prevent a resale market. All they did was corner the market so they can get rich."

Getting rich was the language Cameisha spoke. She knew all too well the hunger pains of being poor. She was ready for some rich people's problems—or so she thought.

"That sucks. Show me how it works," Meisha said, getting up and heading over to the computer. She pulled his wife beater over her head as he slid into his boxers and joined her.

"Let me show you," he said, sitting at the desk. He pulled up his dispensing program and keyed in the password.

Cameisha repeated the word 'sadie' over and over, committing it to memory. She listened intently as he explained the entire operation. He was the last line of defense against fraud. He had to completely verify a company before setting up an account. Once the account was in his system, they could have a variety of pills shipped directly to their office or—even better—P.O. Box.

"So, how much they cost bulk?" Cameisha asked, barely able to conceal her greed and excitement. If it was as easy as he just described, she was about to come up. This would be her hustle, no reason to tell her girls.

"As low as a dollar a pill if they buy a thousand. Small orders are about two fifty, three dollars each," he answered.

"Okay, enough business," she announced, having heard all she needed to hear. She straddled his lap and pulled the t-shirt over her head. "Can I have some more sex, please?"

Bilal's mouth was too full of titty to answer, but that technically is an answer. As he alternated sucking her nipples, he worked his erection through the hole in his boxers. He threw caution to the wind and wriggled inside of her.

Cameisha had never ridden a dick before and let him guide her. He took control and worked her hips in a circular motion until she shook from another orgasm. She was so wet and tight he couldn't help himself from slamming her up and down the length of his pole. Common sense caught up with him just before he came.

"Get up!" he ordered, urgently tapping her on the ass.

Cameisha jumped off and stroked his dick with her hand, making him explode onto his chest and stomach.

Bilal was sleeping two seconds after they hit the bed. That was part of the plan.

Chapter 21

"So, that must be the Mexican she talkin 'bout," Pedro announced, nodding in agreement with himself as he spoke.

Cynthia generously told all of Cameisha's business over the last few weeks. Pedro would hook up with her almost daily and feed her drugs and thug love in exchange for information. He even purchased weed several times through the dingy girl. Her details were so precise. He knew exactly who Juan was when he pulled up to the apartment. She unwittingly set up the robbery Pedro and Big Shawty were planning.

"We should get him right now!" his partner in crime urged.

They already knew the tote bag Juan carried had the weekly ten pound delivery. The dirty duo had been dealing drugs for a decade and never had ten pounds at one time. This would be their biggest lick yet.

The girls, on the other hand, were doing quite well. The ten pounds never made it a full week. They now ran out of weed a day before their re-up. That was partly because people started demanding quarters and ounces. The girls were starting to move weight without even knowing it.

"Chill, shawty, we gone catch him inside and get that money too," Pedro replied.

With ten pounds and five thousand, he could floss real good for a couple of days. A smile pulled his blunt-darkened lips from his gold teeth as another sinister plot entered his corrupt mind. He was going to double up.

"There go yo' girl!" Shawty announced like Pedro couldn't see Cynthia emerge from the building.

"No shit," he shot back. He had sent her to buy the weed she had in her purse in order to follow her. He put the car in gear and pulled off.

****

"Shit!" Bilal shouted as he came.

Cameisha was in front of him on all fours. She had an arch in her back, giving him full access to her goodies. When she collapsed on her stomach, Bilal went with her and landed on her back. This way he got to stay inside of her.

"Mmm, that was good," Meisha purred and massaged him with her vagina muscles. She allowed him to lay there on top and inside until his breathing became heavy. Once his light snores filled the room, she slid from underneath him.

Cameisha stared at him for several minutes before easing out of the bed. She stood up and watched him for another minute before moving again. She had to make sure he was fully asleep because there was no explaining what she was about to do. After taking a deep breath, she tip-toed over to his computer.

"Yes," Meisha cheered in a whisper and pumped her fist when the password granted her access to the program.

She had committed all the particulars to memory and quietly keyed them in. She had set up a company called *The Pain Management Center*. The authentic street address was actually a P.O. Box across town. She verified all the information and approved it.

A pre-paid credit card was set up to pay for the order. She vacillated on whether to order a little just to test it out or go for broke and try to get paid.

"Scared money don't make none," Meisha told herself and placed the order.

Two thousand Oxy pills at two dollars and fifty cent each maxed out the five thousand dollars she put on the card. She was all in and stood to make fifty thousand dollars wholesale. A smile spread on her pretty face when the order was approved. It would ship the next day. Now she had to find a steady supply of customers.

Cameisha felt something as she slid back into bed next to Bilal. It was a twinge of regret, but she was too greedy and selfish to dwell on it.

Instead, she grabbed Bilal by his dick and stroked it while she kissed his face and neck.

"Mmm, round two?" He smiled as he became awake and erect.

It was a silly question, so she didn't bother to answer it. Instead, she climbed on top of him and guided him inside of her. She grabbed his wrists and pinned them to the bed.

"I got this," she commanded and rocked her hips. She got a good stroke going and came with a screech. Meisha rolled off spent, leaving the doctor hanging.

"What about me?" he complained, seeing she was about to go to sleep.

"I got mine, get yours," she shot back and dozed off.

Bilal had no choice but to grab his erection. He used the juice she left behind as lubricant and got his.

Chapter 22

"My boyfriend wants to know if he can buy some pound from you," Cynthia demanded as she barged into the dorm room where Cameisha and Jackie were sleeping. She had the phone to her face ready to relay the answer. Not that she had to, Pedro could hear the conversation just fine.

"Jackie!!" Meisha yelled over to her. Jackie had wanted to be down, so she put her in charge of their burgeoning weight market.

They were running out of weed so quickly now that customers demanded to be able to buy larger quantities. The quality was just fine. They just wanted more of it. Cameisha acquiesced and began selling various amounts up to an ounce. Ounces went for a hundred bucks each. If left to her, Cameisha would have made him buy sixteen of them for the pound.

"I'm up, yo!" Jackie grumbled then turned to Cynthia. "Tell him . . . a stack each."

"A thousand dollars, honey," Cynthia relayed into the phone needlessly. "He said how much if he buy ten?"

"A thousand each," Cameisha interrupted.

"For ten, he can get them for eight," Jackie cut in.

She and Meisha split the proceeds from her sales fifty-fifty, so the $1500 sale was good enough for her. Unlike the boss, she wasn't greedy. She had more money stuffed in her panty drawer now than she ever had in her whole life put together. Even as half of the notorious stick-up kids, Jack and Ill, she rarely saw a coin. Her and her deceased boyfriend caught some sweet licks.

"Okay, he wants ten," Cynthia announced.

Pedro, on the other end, frowned up. He cursed himself for not ordering more since it was that easy.

"But check, it gotta go through you," Jackie stated firmly. "Get the gwap and meet me at the apartment. I aint tryna meet nobody."

"Juan is supposed to come around two. I better hit him and let him know to bring ten more of them things," Cameisha said, sitting up.

"Shit, you need to order another ten for us too," Jackie suggested. She, too, had gotten bit by the hustle bug. Once it hits, it's hard to let it go. Damn near impossible.

"Next time, yo. I'm working on something now where we might be able to cop a hundred of 'em," Meisha said then clammed up before she said too much.

"Okay, he said he gone give me the money," Cynthia said, disconnecting the call. "Shoot, he gone have to break me off at least a pound."

"You know I'ma hit you off for the sale," Jackie replied. She had been paying her ten percent of all the deals she middle-manned. Of course, the pothead always wanted hers in drugs.

When Cynthia left the room, Cameisha stood up and stretched. She stepped into the bathroom to relieve herself then hopped in the shower. Her and Jackie traded places as soon as she stepped out.

"This will do," Meisha told a pair of jeans. She had so many clothes, she kept them in bins under her bed. After pulling the tags off, she squeezed into them.

The weather was funny this time of year, so she selected a tight sweater, choosing to be a little warm over a little cold. She stared ominously at herself in the mirror as she did her hair. That's how Jakcie found her.

"A-yo, what you got going on?" Jackie asked, wrapped in a towel from her own shower.

"Nothing," Cameisha said, snapping out of her trance. She had been sorting out all the 'what ifs' if something went wrong.

"Hold up, let me get dressed. I'm coming with you," she insisted, scrambling for something to put on.

"Chill yo, I got this," Meisha shot back. For all she knew, the police would be waiting on her when she got there. "Just a little experiment. If it goes well, I'll tell you all about it."

Cameisha picked up her phone and hit Juan on the speed dieal.

"Hola, bonita," Juan smiled through the phone. He was becoming very fond of the girl, but it was more sisterly than romantic. He was amused and impressed by her hustle.

"Chillin', papi. Check it, I need to double up today if it's not too late," she sang like girls do when they want something from a boy.

"'Bout time! I was wondering when you was going to move up," he shot back.

Every hustler knows that if your re-ups aren't increasing, something is wrong. That's hustling backwards, and you're in the wrong business.

"No doubt. I need to holla at you later about that," she replied, remembering him saying he needed a pill connect.

"Okay, I'll be there bout two. We can go eat and talk then," he offered.

"Nah, I won't be there. The girls will handle that, and we can talk later."

Cameisha debated whether or not to pack her pistol then decided against it. If the worse case scenario played out, a gun would only make it worse. That would be carrying a pistol in commission of a felony. She shook her head no and walked out of the room.

A bus to the train and then another bus ride later, Cameisha arrived at her destination. She rented the P.O. Box across town to put some distance between her and her crime. She chose this location because it was located in a low crime neighborhood, which meant no need for security cameras.

Meisha walked through the parking lot, scanning all cars then scrutinizing all faces for traces of law enforcement. Satisfied that she saw none, she walked into the business. The way the clerk frowned at her, Cameisha was tempted to turn around and run out. She realized his frown was in response to the one on her face, so she smiled and he smiled back. She found her box and used the key to open it. The smile on her face widened at the sight of the large envelope inside.

Again, she fought the urge to run as she retrieved the package. She wanted to tear into it and pop one on the spot. Instead, she smiled at the clerk again and waved as she walked calmly out of the store.

Cameisha made it all the way back to the bus stop before the feeling got the best of her. She tore a corner off the envelope and poured a pill into her palm. Water would be nice, but since she didn't have any, she summoned some saliva to swallow it down. It took a few tries to get it down. At first it lodged in her throat but eventually went down. By the time Cameisha boarded her train, she was all smiles as the familiar high rang through her being.

Chapter 23

"Get a hint, bitch," Pedro said to his phone as yet another text message came through.

He had stood her up of course. He didn't have a pot to piss in, so he definitely couldn't afford ten pounds. Besides, this was a robbery, and you don't need money for that.

Cynthia had been calling and texting every few seconds. She was strung out on his thug loving as well as weed and was hungry for both.

"Shawty, we finna come up real good off ten pounds of reefer," Big Shawty announced eagerly.

There was no honor among thieves, so Pedro saw no reason to tell him about the extra ten pounds. He hoped he could somehow keep him from knowing about the cash.

"That's him right there," Pedro growled as Juan pulled to a stop. The hater hated the expensive car and nice rims he rolled up in. Then hated the new Jordans he stepped out in, hated his clothes, jewels, and swag.

"That Mexican must be getting it!" Shawty cheered like a groupie. "I got dibs on that chain."

"I want that watch," Pedro called and got out the car.

Both men walked quickly into the building so they could catch Pedro inside. They needed to be in on the deal so they could get both the money and drugs at one time. The ski mask came down to hide their identities from the cameras and victims. This was the point of no return. The guns came out, and they sprinted down the hall. Big Shawty used his big shoulder to open the door.

"What the hell!" Dasia screeched at the intrusion.

"Fuck," Juan sighed and shook his head.

Masked men with guns at a drug deal meant the same all over the world. This was a robbery, and he got caught slipping. Usually, there would be security, or at least a gun in his waistband, but not today.

"Shut the fuck up! Y'all know what time it is," Big Shawty yelled, scanning the room with his gun. He made sure each and every occupant got a chance to look down the huge barrel of the 45.

"I'll take this," Pedro announced as he scooped the neatly-stacked money from the coffee table. He turned to Juan and stared.

Juan frowned at the odd move. If it was a robbery, take the loot and flee. This was personal. He lifted the bag containing the weed to hand it over. Pedro snatched it but kept staring.

"You fucking her, ain't you?" Pedro demanded.

Juan looked over at Dasia and Aqua, assuming he meant one of them.

"Fuck you doing, shawty?" Big Shawty demanded. "Get that nigga's jewels so we can get the fuck outta here."

"Yeah, you fucking her. Don't lie."

"Here you go, man," Juan said smoothly as he took off the diamond-studded PJS medallion and chain. He handed it over then his watch and ring. "I'm not touching the girls. I have a fiancé."

"Lying ass nigga. I should bust yo' ass," Pedro growled.

Juan could see he was building himself up to shout and saw no reason to wait. He threw a quick upper cut that sent Pedro backpeddling as he dashed for the door. Juan reached for the door knob as Pedro recovered and fired. Two slugs tore into his back and dropped him to the floor. Both Dasia and Aqua fled to the rear as Big Shawty ran for the door. He hopped over Juan and tore down the hallway.

"Keep yo' hands off my bitch," Pedro told Juan as he stepped over him. He pointed the pistol at his face and fired once more.

****

"Whoa! Whoa! Slow down," Cameisha barked into her phone as she took the frantic call. As soon as she took the call, Dasia launched into one long word about the robbery.

"I said we got hit. Two niggas just ran up in here and robbed us. They shot Juan," she got out.

"He's dead?" Cameisha asked and held her breath for an answer. "They still there?"

"I don't know. It just happened. We ran to the back."

"Okay, get all drug-related shit out now. Have Aqua take scales, money, bags, everything and go to the dorm. Police gonna come so say he was your man and someone came in and shot him. Don't say shit about drugs," Meisha directed.

"Okay, I got it. You coming over?" Dasia asked hopefully.

"Nah, call me once the cops leave," she replied.

She certainly couldn't go to a crime scene with ten thousand Oxy pills in her purse. Actually, one thousand nine hundred and ninety nine because one was coursing through her system making her feel great.

The police arrived shortly after Aqua fled with all drug paraphernalia. In this area, where robberies were common place, it was quickly labeled as such. Juan was alert when loaded into an ambulance but didn't answer any questions.

Dasia stuck to the script and played the worried girlfriend. She was questioned for a few minutes but couldn't provide much information either. Two masked men kicked the door in and started shouting. The cops knew it was more to it but didn't really care. They loaded up their gear and went off to the next crime scene. This was Atlanta after all; they had plenty to keep them busy.

It was well into the evening when Cameisha finally made it to the hospital. She knew the shooting would have detectives hovering around. There were no detectives when she arrived but a slew of angry looking Spanish men.

The observant girl counted no less than four cars in the parking lot. The way the men scanned and scrutinized everyone who passed—including her—she knew they were security. But why was the question that contorted her pretty face.

The answer was because the Salazars were big time royalty among Columbian drug dealers. They moved their operation to America fifteen years ago. The mother of the clan was queen, but the recent college graduate, Uan, was the brains.

Two more Columbian men in suits analyzed Cameisha as she stepped into the hospital. A quick once over from her revealed the guns they concealed under their suit jackets. It was then she realized Juan was larger than he claimed to be. He made it appear as if he had a connect, but it was now clear that he was the connect.

The private room was full of family all speaking rapid fire Spanish at once. Juan couldn't speak because his jaw had been broken from the last shot Pedro fired into his face. It was wired shut and swollen the size of a melon. The other two bullets passed harmlessly through his body, missing vital organs.

Cameisha listened from the door for a minute and translated that she was the topic of conversation. The thought to turn around and leave crossed her mind, but she was free from blame and went in to clear her name.

"I knew that girl couldn't be trusted. I bet you she is behind this," Uan's woman declared in Spanish. She had witnessed him laughing and smiling too much when speaking to the girl for comfort.

"If that were the case, then why am I here?" Meisha asked in Spanish as she stepped in the room.

"Odios Mio!" Juan's mother, Marisol, exclaimed and covered her mouth as if she saw a ghost when she looked at the intruder.

Everyone stared in shocked silence at the woman's reactions. Cameisha shrugged it off and walked over to Juan.

"Como esta?" she asked, offering a sympathetic smile.

Juan offered as much of a smile as someone shot in the face could and nodded. He pulled his hand free from Angela's and reached for Cameisha's.

"I'm going to find out who did this and take care of it," she assured him.

Those in the room who were fluent in murder heard the rest of the statement. Like they say, what's understood doesn't need to be explained.

The Salazar brothers were amused by the tough talk of the young girl. They murmured at her murderous declarations until the matriarch spoke up.

"What is your name?" Marisol requested, sounding like a woman use to making demands.

"Cameisha," Cameisha replied, turning around to give the woman her full attention.

"Where you from? Your parents?" she questioned, still wearing the discriminating frown.

"Mississippi. My daddy from Mexico."

"Well, Cameisha, this whole business is very disturbing to me. My son being shot. You double your order, and a robber is waiting?" Marisol said, putting her assumptions in the air for all to see.

Juan shook his head no from his bed.

Cameisha's mouth dropped open from the truth of the statement. Two plus two equals four in every language on the globe. The room grew eerily quiet as she did the mental math. Cynthia's boyfriend was behind this, no question. Meisha's pretty face turned red with murder as she wondered if Cynthia was involved. No one had ever seen the mystery man, and now it was obvious that his frequent buys were designed to see how deep the water ran.

"God as my witness, I am not involved," Cameisha said, walking face-to-face with the diamond-studded woman. She couldn't help but notice that she was fly even at a time like this. Emergency or no emergency, her hair, face, and clothes were perfect. "But because it happened on my watch, I will pay for it. Remember, I lost too though. I have a connect for Oxy. I can let them go for ten dollars each and they . . ."

"Five dollars each," Marisol corrected. It was her way of negotiating.

"Like I said, five dollars a piece. I have two . . . um, one thousand nine hundred of them, so that will pay for your product," Meisha said, deciding to keep a hundred pills for her own personal use. "And I will personally handle whoever did this."

"Mmm mm," Juan mumbled urgently, getting everyone's attention. He made movements with his hand as if writing.

"Here, baby," Angela purred, handing him a pen and pad from her designer purse.

He took it and quickly scribbled one word. When he finished, he extended it to his mother. Marisol crossed the room in regal steps and took the paper. A smile spread on her face as she read then she leaned in and kissed his forehead.

"Qisas," she read aloud for the benefit of everyone in attendance.

The brothers all smiled and nodded too.

"I'm not familiar with that word?" Cameisha frowned. Her Spanish was fluent with a faux Puerto Rican accent from her high school teacher's homeland.

"It's an Arabic word," Marisol explained. "It means the law of equality, an eye for an eye. When you find who did this, you must let Juan have revenge."

"Are you sure 'cause I have this uncle called Killa and . . ."

"Qisas!" Marisol repeated.

Chapter 24

"Okay, tell me again what they looked like," Cameisha growled in a low murderous tone. She knew exactly who the gunmen were from the first description but wanted to hear it again.

"They both had on ski masks, but the stubby one had a hole for his mouth, and he had gold teeth with one missing," Aqua repeated.

"Yeah, but the tall one was running the show," Dasia added. "A-yo, why that one was saying Juan touched his girl? Wait . . . y'all fucking?"

"I knew it! I knew it!" Aqua joined in. "'Cause when he come over you be all 'Hey, papi', and he be all 'Sup, mama'. I knew it!"

"They do too! She be all girly and shit," Dasi recalled and slapped high fives with Aqua.

"Damn, you ain't said shit to me about it." Jackie pouted.

"That's 'cause we ain't fucking! Never mind all that, we tryna figure who robbed us," Cameisha said embarrassed.

She was no doubt smitten by the suave Latino, but he had a woman, and she was too proud to be a side chick and too smart to covet what she could not have. It was true; Juan was very affectionate towards her, but it was sisterly, not romantic.

"Yo, it's definitely Pedro and his mutt Shawty, but what Cynthia got to do with them?" Cameisha frowned.

"She seem cool. I can't see her setting us up," Aqua stated.

"I'm about to go beat that bitch until she tell me," Jackie said, standing. Had Cameisha not stopped her, she would have marched over to the dorm and done just that.

"I just can't see it, yo. I can't see her turning on us," Meisha pondered.

There was no doubt that Cynthia's drug buy was involved in the robbery. Pedro knew exactly when, where, and how much. Cynthia was an airhead and liked to get high. That made her vulnerable bait, prey but not treacherous.

"Pedro is slimy enough to use her to get at me," Meisha concluded. Her mind flashed to their pillow talk and petty schemes.

Aqua shrugged. "You should just call you uncle."

"For real! Killa come down here and air that whole shit out," Dasia seconded.

"Nah yo, this my beef, and I'll handle it," she replied as if she hadn't thought of it herself. "Besides, we gotta save Pedro for Juan."

"What about Cynthia?" Jackie demanded. "What we gone do about her?"

"Nothing. Don't do nothing, don't say nothing. We gonna use her to set him up, just like he did us. And if I do find out she was down with that shit, I'ma kill her myself."

****

Later that night, Cynthia joined the crew in Cameisha's dorm room for a smoke session. Cynthia never missed a free get high, even if she was already high. She was too deep in her own little world to catch the intense vibe in the room. Aqua, Dasia, and Jackie all glared dangerously at her as she rambled on.

"Girl, I told him to suck his own dick. Shoot, he don't wanna eat no cooch so—"

"Dang, my phone off. Let me use yours real quick," Meisha asked, cutting in on Cynthia's recounting of last night's sexcapades. She passed the blunt to sweeten the deal.

"Sure! That happens to me all the time," Cynthia said, taking the bait and passing the phone. She switched the topic of conversation from sex to cell phones.

This was plan B to get a hold of Cynthia's phone. Jackie suggested getting it at gunpoint, but a blunt worked better. Cameisha went through her phone while she tried to smoke as much as she could before she had to pass it.

The first stop was the picture gallery. She quickly scrolled past pictures of Cynthia's breasts and vagina. She was scrolling so fast that she had to back up when she saw a familiar penis. It had the same fat head and squiggly vein running the length of the thick shaft. The tatted up torso had the same crude ink but then came Pedro's face. He pulled his lips into a grimace to show off his gold teeth and smokey black gums. The name on the pictures said 'Dre', so she checked the contacts to find it. Knowing the number by heart, Cameisha had no problem identifying it.

The thought of killing Cynthia crossed her mind again now that she had confirmation that she was the link to getting them robbed. When she pulled up the text messages, it saved her life. She saw all the text pleading with him to call or hit back on the day of the robbery and changed her mine.

"Here you go. Thanks." Meisha smiled and handed the phone back.

"Um . . . okay . . . no . . . problem," Cynthia said between pulls on the blunt.

Everyone looked at Cameisha for confirmation. She gave it to them by nodding up and down as Cynthia moved on to the next topic. Once the blunt was finished, she was ready to go.

"Well, let me get a bag for the road," she asked, further proving she was unaware of the robbery.

"We out right now, give us a day or so," Jackie replied and opened the door for her.

Cynthia had been put out of the room enough to know that was her cue. She made her goodbyes and was off in search of another session.

"A-yo, Jackie, chill here. We finna go to the projects just to have a look around," Cameisha said, sliding a clip into her little 380 pistol.

"Thought you 'posed to save dude for dude?" Jackie asked.

"I am. Just going to have a look around," Meisha replied like she believed it herself.

"So, I guess that's binoculars then, huh?" she asked about the gun. "How you gone see something in the rain anyway?"

The light rain and early winter dusk provided a nice disguise as they slipped into the projects. They huddled under one umbrella and walked briskly. Cameisha's first stop came up empty as Pedro's donk wasn't parked in front of his apartment.

"Let's see if his boy home," Meisha suggested and led them to the building. Pedro had either dropped Big Shawty off or picked him up.

Since she wasn't sure exactly which unit he lived in, they posted up in front of the corner store. Cameisha picked up the pay phone and pretended to talk while they staked out Shawty's building.

"How them things work anyway?" Aqua wondered. Hers was the cell phone generation, so they never used pay phones before.

"I think you gotta put money in it," Dasia guessed since she had never used one before either.

"That's him!" Aqua said urgently as Big Shawty stepped from an apartment.

"Yeah, it is," Dasia agreed, sealing his fate. "We need a plan."

"Yeah, a plan." Meisha masked and walked away leaving them standing in the rain. She tilted the umbrella forward to conceal her face as she approached. She was still mumbling about a plan as Shawty popped the truck to fix one of the new amps he bought with his share of her money.

"Meisha!" Dasia demanded through clenched teeth. Even if Cameisha did hear her, she wouldn't have heard her because she had murder on her mind.

Big Shawty heard footsteps and looked up just in time to see Cameisha raise the gun. Before he could say a word, fire exploded from the tip, sending a copper bullet speeding towards his face. A last second flinch saved his life, but only for a few seconds as the shot at his temple slammed into his jaw.

Shawty had been shot at and shot enough times in life to know to run. He turned to flee and took three rounds in his back, one for every step he took. The gun in his pocket was useless because there was no time to pull it as he fell to the pavement. He rolled over to plea for his life just in time to see the look on his killer's face just before she killed him. At least it was a smile.

An evil grin would probably describe it better. Cameisha fired one last shot into his forehead and then kicked him. She turned quickly and took off running. Dasia and Aqua took off too from across the street. They crossed over and joined the sprint back to the dorm.

"Chill, chill," Cameisha ordered and slowed to a walk just before they got to the main street.

When the shots rang out in the war-torn projects, no one looked to see who was shooting. Instead, the battle-weary residents took cover under beds and in bathtubs. This would be just another murder in the projects.

"What did yo' crazy ass do?" Jackie squinted as they returned. She couldn't hear the shots, but Cameisha had her 'murder mami' face on, and Aqua was still huffing and puffing from the run.

"Nothing." Meisha smiled innocently then came clean. "One down."

Chapter 25

Having cake certainly has its advantage. And being that the Salazar family was caked the fuck up, Juan was able to recuperate at home. A team of doctors and nurses were dispatched to the family mansion to keep tabs on him. Of course, Angela hovered around at all times. She accused all the nurses of flirting with him and cursed one out for taking his temperature.

Juan would have preferred to go to his own condo, but Mama Salazar wasn't hearing it. The best he could manage was staying in the pool house. Once he got settled good, he sent for Cameisha so they could complete their arrangement.

Remembering the security in the parking lot at the hospital, Cameisha knew the tinted-out Range Rover pulling onto the block was her ride.

"Sure you don't want me to come, yo?" Jackie asked fearfully.

"I'm cool, ma. I'm like part of the family." Meisha smiled and replied far more confidently than she felt. They had tossed the dirty gun in the dumpster, but even if she had it, what good would it do.

When the truck stopped in front of her, she walked to the curb and stopped. Grandma said divas do not open doors, so she waited. She didn't have to wait long as the burly Columbian driver got out and rushed around the front of the range to open the door. He even assisted her gently by the elbow as she stepped into the vehicle. Once she was seated, he closed it and got in. Meisha and Jackie locked eyes as the truck pulled off.

Cameisha was shocked at how quickly and thoroughly the landscape changed once they reached the suburbs. The town of Vinings was a stone's throw from the city but a world away. Every vehicle that passed by was above the fifty thousand dollar range and nothing over a few years old. In this world, cars get traded in for new ones after two or three years. Then niggas buy them, put big ass rims on them, and floss. Like they say: one man's trash . . .

Manicured lawns hid behind wrought iron gates on both sides of the street. Had this been an actual tour, the guide would have been pointing out various homes of celebrities and businessmen. The gate that the driver pulled up to was opened as he approached. Cameisha gasped at the sight of the fancy mansion at the end of a driveway full of fancy cars.

"Senor Juan is in the pool house," the driver announced as if practicing his English.

Cameisha smiled and thanked him in perfect Spanish, causing him to smile proudly. He pointed at the pool house as he helped her down from the vehicle. She followed where he pointed and walked into the backyard.

"Hola, Cameisha!" Marisol called from where she and Angela were seated on the patio. Cameisha pasted a smile on her face and walked over to pay her respects to the lady of the house. "Como esta?"

"Fine and you?" Meisha replied and asked sweetly.

They engaged in small talk while Angela checked her up and down with a frown.

"Juan is expecting you," Marisol advised once the niceties were out of the way. She pointed at the pool house which was a miniature two bedroom replica of the main house.

Cameisha bid her farewell and went to see Juan. She could feel daggers being thrown at her back as she walked away.

"There is something about her," Marisol wondered, squinting as if that would somehow bring it in focus.

"I don't trust her," Angela stated needlessly.

"You Trust No Bitch like Cash and Nene." Madam Salazar laughed.

"Nope," Angela said and got up to follow Cameisha in.

"Sup, Papi?" Meisha smiled when she walked in on Juan playing video games with one of his brothers.

"Sup wit' chu?" he gritted back from behind his wired jaw and paused the game.

Brother Carlos smiled, nodded, and excused himself.

"Aww, let me see," Meisha moaned at the sight of the large bandage on his cheek. She went to touch it, and that's exactly how Angela found her when she walked in.

"Do you have a boyfriend?" she asked, sitting practically on his hip.

"Yes." Cameisha smiled as Bilal's smile flashed in her mind. She hadn't seen or spoken to him since the robbery. He had been leaving voicemails and text messages but she was too preoccupied to reply.

"Do you like for strange women to touch his face?" Angela asked curtly.

"I'm not strange. I'm family. This is my big brother," Meisha said still rubbing his bandage.

Angela frowned. She would remember this statement later when it proved true. She was going to frown then too.

"Mmm," Juan grimaced from the pain of her touch.

"My bad, yo. You might want to keep a few of these yourself," Cameisha offered as she passed him the package containing 1,900 Oxy pills.

"Never that! Drugs are for drug addicts," he shot back. "These are sold already at ten bucks each. I need more, like ten thousand."

"At five dollars!" Meisha cheered at the hefty profit.

"Yeah, right." Juan laughed and frowned from the pain of laughing. "Three," he said, holding up three fingers.

"That's what's up. I'm not sure if I can get that many at once though." She thought for a second then said, "Let's do five and five, three fifty a piece. If that works out, we'll try the ten."

"Okay, your stuff is in the bag," he gritted, referring to a totebag on the table.

Cameisha wasn't expecting anything and frowned as she went to investigate.

"Ay-yo, my money fucked up right now," she said, seeing the bag was full of weed—ten pounds of compressed bricks.

"The pills put us even. We have a clean slate," Juan said, causing Angela to suck her pretty teeth and walk out. "Sup with our mutual friends?"

"Um . . . see . . . okay, one died, but I saved one for you," Meisha stammered.

"Died? From what?"

"My gun. Which reminds me, I need another one."

"Yes, you do. A twenty-two?" he underestimated.

"No. Glock forty, please. My favorite!"

Chapter 26

Saturday night rolled around and the whole crew had dates. Cynthia met up with Pedro for hard drugs and rough sex. Even though he was still flush with cash from the robbery, he still made her spend daddy's dough. He would charge her for the weed smoked and the coke that was becoming more frequent. The slimeball decided to raise the stakes and push her further into his pocket.

"What's that?" Cynthia asked curiously as Pedro dropped several small baggies on the hotel table. She picked one up and marveled at the small rock inside.

"Primo," he replied evasively and split a cigar.

He dumped the guts out and replaced it with some of the stolen weed. Cynthia watched curiously as he crushed one of the rocks and laced the blunt. Using his tart saliva, he sealed the cigar and lit it. The blunt sparked and sizzled as he inhaled.

"Hmp," Pedro said, passing the blunt. He quickly blew the smoke out before it could affect him. One, because he planned on using his dick, and two, because he didn't smoke crack.

Cynthia did though. She immediately felt the life-changing effects of the blunt. It felt as if she were actually floating, so she took another and another. The brand new junky was happy Pedro never asked for the weed back and let her smoke. Once she had her fill, he led her to the bed to fill her up.

Coke always made her horny, but after smoking crack, it was extra. This is why crack whores worked such long shifts. Dick and dope equals win/win. Pedro shoved his erection in her face as usual, and she finally opened up.

Aqua was going out with her football player again. The future sports star would one day be a millionaire, but he was dead broke now. But, like they say, it ain't tricking if you got it, and Aqua had it. She generously sprung for movies and the huge meals they ate. After all, business was booming, and the girls kept pockets full of money.

The large couple hit the mall earlier and shopped for his and hers outfits. Surf and turf filled their bellies then off to the movies. Once the credits rolled, it was off to the dorms for sex.

Since it was Dasia's turn to hold down the fort, she was stuck alone in the apartment. There was the usual Saturday night rush of people wanting their weed for the evening then the slow down.

"I need a man," Dasia said aloud.

She was attempting to shake thoughts of Lisa out of her mind. The thoughts that had her panties soaked as she recalled the night she spent wit her and the rapper. The coke and oral sex were the highlights of the night. When the throbbing between her legs became too much, she made the call.

An hour later, Lisa was making lines of cocaine on the coffee table. She picked up a gram of mediocre coke on the way over, and Dasia supplied the wine coolers and weed. They listened to music and made small talk until the coke was snorted, blunt was smoked, and glasses empty.

"What now?" Dasia asked fearfully. She wanted the girl to touch her but didn't know how to say it. She wore a tiny skirt and braless wife beater for her as bait, hoping she would bite or at least lick.

"What do you want to happen?" Lisa asked and scooted next to her on the sofa. She palmed her exposed thigh and stared straight into her inner being. The part of the eye where truth is kept and asked, "Do you want me to eat your pussy?"

"Y . . . ye . . . yesss," Dasia managed to get out as Lisa's hand moved under the skirt.

"I see!" Lisa giggled when her hand reached the wet panties. She pulled them aside and slid a finger inside of her. She leaned in to kiss her, and they made out while she played in her pussy.

Lisa stopped just short of making Dasia cum and pulled her hand away. She silently stood and peeled off her tight jeans. Dasia took the hint and leaned back to come out of her skirt and panties. Once they were naked, Lisa positioned her for a sixty-nine and lowered her throbbing box onto her mouth.

Dasia came almost instantly after Lisa clamped her mouth onto her vagina. She sucked her to an orgasm a minute later. The girls ate pussy until they were both full and came several times each. When they sat up, they kissed and tasted their own juices off each other's mouths.

"Can we get more coke?" someone asked.

"Sure, I'll call my people," Lisa replied and reached for her phone.

Dasia was shocked that the question came from her, but since it was in the air, she didn't try to take it back.

"You like?" Bilal asked needlessly as Cameisha shoveled food into her mouth.

"What? This shit is delicious, yo," Cameisha cheered with her mouth full. She had smoked weed with her crew, in addition to popping a pill, and was super hungry and horny.

"My mom's recipe." Bilal smiled proudly. "Glad you like it."

Luckily, he came for the empty plate before she had a chance to lap up the rest of the sauce with her tongue. Cameisha smiled as she watched him clear the table and load the dishwasher. She was too horny to wait for him to clean the kitchen, so she took matters into her own hands. While he worked, she quickly stripped out of her outfit and climbed on the table.

"How about some desert?" she called.

When Bilal turned his head in her direction, she seductively spread her legs. He did a double take and rushed over. He retook his seat and marvelled at the shaved vagina in front of him. After spending all day at work fixing beat-up boxes, this fresh and clean pussy was a treat. Treats are to be eaten, so he leaned in and tasted it. He had her so close to an orgasm by touching it; it exploded and sprayed his face the second his tongue touched it.

He stood and frantically freed the erection from his pants and plunged inside of her raw. It was so intense, and she was so wet, so tight, so good.

"Shit!" Bilal didn't last a full minute before snatching himself out and spewing warm gobs of semen all the way up to her neck.

"Come on!" he shouted and pulled Cameisha up from the table. Bilal rushed her into his room and onto the bed and pushed back inside of her.

There would be no quick nut this time. Bilal pulled Cameisha's legs up and opened by her ankles and fucked her. She grabbed fistfuls of the sheets and gritted her teeth to take the pounding. One hour and eight positions later, Bilal pulled out and skeeted on her back.

Once he was empty, he slumped over on the bed, breathing heavily. Cameisha rolled over to face him and traded soft pecks.

"I see somebody missed me." She giggled between kisses.

"I did, but I understand. Mid-terms can be brutal," he said, indicating that he bought her excuse.

"Yeah, mid-terms," she repeated the lie.

The truth was that she missed her mid-terms dealing with the robbery. She was supposed to have been in computer lab at the exact moment she put a bullet in Big Shawty's big head.

Cameisha rubbed Bilal's face softly as he blinked sleep into view. He smiled as he tried to fight it, but eventually, the sandman got his man. She waited a while until his soft snores grew louder and slipped out of the bed. She stood over him and watched him for a minute before creeping over to the computer.

"Shit!" Meisha shouted in a whisper as the computer beeped loudly when it came to life. She scrambled to turn the volume down.

Using her own personal money, she ordered five thousand pills at two dollars each. It was a gamble, but she took the risk. She couldn't gamble with the crew's money, but if it succeeded, she planned to put them on too.

The order was approved and set for delivery in two days. After shutting the program and then computer down, she slid back in bed and snuggled up next to Bilal.

Chapter 27

Cameisha knew she was slipping in school and buckled down. She took make-up exams and managed to pass. Things were running smoothly enough for her to fall back and concentrate on her classes.

A knock on the door startled both her and Jackie.

"You expecting someone?" she asked Jackie.

"Yeah, Samantha wants an ounce," she replied and went to open the door.

Jackie now handled the weight sales, selling anything from an ounce to a quarter pound. It was far less traffic than the dime bags handled at the apartment.

Samantha was one of the few white kids attending the predominantly black school. While the other whites were 'wiggers' or black wanna bes, she was a pure white girl. She loved black men, so over her parent's objections, she chose the black school. They tried to squeeze her into a white school by cutting off her funds, but the brilliant chemistry student got grants, scholarships, and finally, a job in the school's lab.

"Sup, Sam. This my roommate, Meisha," Jackie said as she let the customer in.

Cameisha fought a frown from forming on her face at the introduction. She hated meeting new people. New people meet new problems, and she was content with her small circle of friends, a circle that started out larger. The ones who were left were the survivors—the loyal ones.

Samantha smiled, took a deep breath, and went in.

"Hey, Cameisha. I'm Samantha, but Jackie just told you that. Oh my gosh, you are so pretty. You look like this girl I grew up with back home in Ohio. Have you ever been to Ohio? It's okay. I've never been to New York but can't wait to go. There was a guy from New York who came to my school in twelfth grade. All the black girls hated me when we started dating. They wanted to fight me everyday. I got my ass kicked so many times; I just broke up with him."

Cameisha shot Jackie an 'is she serious?' glance as Samantha rambled on. Jackie just shrugged and continued her task. She held the ounce of weed on the hand scale so Samantha could see she was getting what she paid for. That was a lesson the dope girl learned from her dope boy father and passed on to her crew. They always gave proper weight. The tiny dime sacks were what the market allowed, but if you paid for an ounce, you got an ounce. Samantha nodded her approval so she wouldn't have to stop talking.

"Oh, did I tell you guys about my new experiment? I took an acidic powder and increased its weight four times without losing any of the properties. It was as potent as the original. Simple really, I just found the right combination of melamine and added electrons."

"Is that right?" Jackie asked as they traded weed for cash.

She guided her to the door, opened it, and ushered her out into the hall while she was still talking. Someone else was going to catch the rest of that story.

"Hey, y'all!" Cynthia sang, barging in before Jackie could get the door closed all the way. "Got weed?"

"Hey, Cynthia, yeah we straight," Jackie replied dryly.

"Smoke one then," she cheered.

"No doubt," Meisha replied, shaking her head at Jackie before she could flip on her. "So how yo' man doing?"

"Who Dre? He cool, posed to link up with him later," she said.

Cameisha fed her a blunt and let her ramble on, telling all his business.

She gleamed that Pedro didn't even attend Big Shawty's funeral. What she didn't know was that his slimy ass broke into their apartment and robbed them while the family was burying him.

"Y'all still ain't got no blow? Y'all need to get some coke. Everybody wants coke," Cynthia announced.

"She ain't lying. I get asked every time somebody cop weed," Jackie added.

Cameisha only nodded, but she was hearing that a lot lately.

Dasia had been campaigning that they sold blow as well. While it was true that several customers requested it daily, she was developing a taste for it herself. She and Lisa linked up a few times, snorting and eating the night away.

"I might just have to get a package. Something small just to see what's happening," she relented. She almost believed it herself.

Cocaine changed the dynamics of the game. It put different players on the field and most didn't play fair. Sure, it was more money, but with that comes more problems.

"Say, Cynthia, give me a ride to . . . nah, forget it," Meisha started and stopped. It would have cut two hours in travel time getting a ride versus taking the bus, but Cynthia couldn't hold water.

Need my own car, she thought as the bus rumbled to her destination. "You ain't got no license," she replied aloud to the thought.

Once again, she was on high alert as she made her way through the parking lot to the P.O. Box. If she got away clean this time, she would try them up for ten thousand pills and the fifteen thousand dollar payday.

"Money is more addictive than any drug," her father's voice reminded.

"I know, Daddy. I got this," she told his memory.

****

Angela sucked her teeth and rolled her eyes when she pulled the condo door open and saw who rang the bell. Not wanting to get in trouble, she stepped aside so the guest could enter. The driver-slash-bodyguard, Manny, stood with a scowl that quickly turned into a smile.

"I'm fine, thank you. And you?" Cameisha tensed as she stepped inside. "Hola, Manny, como esta usted? Bien, que es mi hermano?" she replied, causing Angela to suck her teeth again.

Angela frowned and pointed to the den. She was too jealous to even let her man have a sister. Cameisha couldn't help but admire her outfit as she stormed off.

"Hey, Mamacita," Juan gritted through his wired jaw but still managed to smile.

"Sup, big bruh?" Meisha replied with her own smile and tossed him the bag of pills.

"You 'bout ready to step up again, huh?" he asked, knowing she knocked off ten pounds in four days.

"Yeah, that's what I need to talk to you about," she said sheepishly. She knew she was about to cross a line with what she was about to say, so she inhaled a deep breath, exhaled, and then crossed it.

"I need some coke. Not a lot, just enough for a few customers then I'm done."

"You really believe that?" Juan grimaced. Had she said yes, he wouldn't have given her any. That would mean she was far too naïve for the cocaine trade.

"No," Meisha twisted her lips and admitted. "So many people asking for it. I can't keep letting all that money get by me."

"That's the curse of a hustla. So, what we talking, a key? Two?" Juan asked.

"Nah, a couple ounces should do. It's just for the kids at school."

"No problem. Are you still riding the bus with drugs?" He frowned.

"Sure. I'm a college kid with a book bag." Cameisha laughed. It was foolish but worked, as police never gave her a second glance, except to check out her ass.

"You need a car. I'm gonna give you a car. You can pay me when you get the money," he said, adding the last part knowing the proud girl wouldn't take it otherwise.

"I can't drive," she admitted with her head lowered.

"Manny! Ouch," Juan yelled then grimaced from the pain. He rubbed his sore jaw as the driver rushed in to answer his summons. "Wires come out next week."

"Yes, boss," Manny said, appearing in the doorway.

"Teach my sister to drive. Let her drive to her house then deliver my white car from the yellow house," Juan instructed.

"No problem, boss," the obedient man replied and took his leave.

"You have your eyes on our two friends," Juan asked, managing a vindictive smile.

"Umm, like I said before, it's only one left," Meisha admitted like a child about to be scolded.

"What happened to the other one?" he asked, not believing her the first time she mentioned it.

"I shot him in his head. I saved one for you though," she said proudly.

"You are too much." Juan laughed shaking his head.

Chapter 28

When Cameisha got to the apartment, she gave the large package of weed to Aqua to start bagging up. She would make quarters and dimes for the apartment and separate ounces for Jackie.

Dasia watched Cameisha curiously as she removed items from the local head shop that sold items for freaks and drug dealers. She and Lisa had just been picking up accessories for their freaky session.

Instead of a two-headed dildo or pina colada pussy gel, lactose and a digital scale came out of the bag. Next came all things needed to package cocaine for street-level distribution.

"I see smart ass sent an eight instead of an ounce," Cameisha grumbled when she pulled the cocaine out of the bag. She weighed it by eye, accurately guessing the four and half ounces.

Dasia felt her stomach churn at the sight of the cocaine. She could smell it through the bag, and when it hit the table, it was all she could do not to drop her face into the pile and inhale. She knew that was against the rules because cocaine use and cocaine sales didn't go well together.

"A-yo. This shit so pure, we can cut it in half and still have the best blow around," Cameisha marveled at the glistening fish scale.

Cocaine gets stepped on at every step it makes coming to market. By the time it reaches nostrils, its usually cut to oblivion. Twenty to thirty percent pure at best but getting it directly from the horse's mouth meant one hundred percent pure cocaine.

"Measure out four—no three—ounces of cut," she ordered and started putting chunks of coke into a grinder.

Dasia complied and took out three ounces of lactose and put it on the table. She began folding it into the powder an hour into the mixing, that ensured a good quality.

The door bell rang.

"Yo, get that," Cameisha told Aqua, who quickly got up.

"Shh!!" Juan shushed, holding a finger to his lips, wearing a mischievous smile. "Come on."

Aqua smiled and crept out behind him to see what he was up to. She saw the surprise when she got outside and went back to get her.

"A-yo, Meisha, come out here," Aqua said, sticking her head in the door. She quickly retreated before Cameisha could question her.

"This girl probably seen a damn butterfly." She sighed and got up.

The exact second the door closed behind her, Dasia scooped a heap of coke in each nostril.

"The fuck!" she exclaimed when the superior-grade coke hit her throat. It was a far cry from the stuff Lisa brought over. That shit had more cuts than a DJ battle.

Moving quickly, she removed half an ounce of the mixture then mixed in another half ounce of lactose. Even still, it would crush the competition.

"Oh my God! That's me?" Cameisha clapped when she saw Juan sitting on a nearly-new Acura.

"Yup," he replied, tossing her the keys. "No driving until you get your license though."

"I did good, tell him Manny," she cheered.

"She did," Manny cosigned honestly.

Like most things she tried, Cameisha picked up on driving immediately. She merely mimicked what she'd seen for years and followed Manny's directions.

"Oh and what's up with that o-z?" Meisha asked, twisting her lips.

"Either you in or you out. Don't play with it," Juan said, answering the question about the extra coke. He didn't want her fooling herself and running back and forth flipping ounces. That was junky logic, buying twenties all night. Why not keep it real with yourself and spend what you're going to spend.

"You ready to run that 10k race?" he asked, requesting his ten thousand Oxy pills.

"Yup. Couple of days. It'll probably take 'til the weekend to finish," she grossly underestimated.

"See you then," Juan agreed.

He accepted a hug from Meisha and Dasia before joining Manny in the range.

****

"Wow! This shit is that shit!" Cynthia cheered as she hit the blow. Cameisha had given her one of the 180, one gram fifties they bagged.

After paying Juan two thousand for the coke, they would profit seven grand. It would be evenly split between the whole crew.

"Told ya," Meisha said proudly. "Spread the word but it goes through you."

"Give me another!" Cynthia demanded and produced a fifty dollar bill from her purse. "Got a hot date tonight."

"With . . . um . . . what's his name again?" Jackie asked, trying her up. The moment she let on that Dre was Dro, she was going to kill her.

"His"—snort—"name"—snort—"is"—snort—"Dre," she replied between snorts. "He's taking me somewhere special tonight."

****

"This is the special place I told you about," Pedro said proudly as he led Cynthia into his first apartment.

"Don't look so special to me," Jackie quipped as she drove past them. Since she already had her license, she drove while they tailed him.

"Bum ass nigga," Meisha snarled. She hated him for all his treachery but watching him palm Cynthia's ass as he led her inside added to her feelings. She knew first hand that a good dicking down waited inside. "Can't wait 'til Juan murders his ass."

"Let me find out you jealous about a dead man and a junky! Let me find out," Jackie said as she pulled off.

Before leaving the run-down apartment complex, Jackie drove around to scope the place out. They took note of both entrances and exits, as well as a security guard driving around looking for trouble. Trouble was coming, too, more than he could handle.

Inside the apartment, Pedro asked subtle questions about Cameisha, letting the dimwit snort, smoke, and drink. She could only relay false information the girls fed her. He was able to gleam that Meisha had access to the good coke Cynthia produced. He refrained from taking a hit since he had plans for his dick.

Cynthia had plans for it too. She pulled it free from his sweaty boxers and kissed it fully erect. Then she put hits of coke on it and either snorted or sucked it off. Pedro's dick was hard and numb when he led her into the spare bedroom. An air mattress was the only furniture in the room, but that's all that was needed. He fucked her every which way but loose as plans were made to end his miserable life. Qisas!

Chapter 29

Once the team made the jump to coke, there was no turning back. Coke heads came from every direction for the superior grade product—athletes, cool kids, and even the nerds. The coke sold so fast it scared Cameisha. Making that much money that fast is a life-changing experience. It's as addictive as the blast of a crack pipe and just as powerful.

Everyone agreed to invest a part of their earnings to get more coke. Cameisha was the boss, but the operation was a cooperative that shared all profits equally. Of course, that only works if nobody gets greedy or strung out.

Juan played his role as watchful big brother and gave them a generous four thousand dollar ticket for nine ounces of ninety percent cocaine. If they sold it raw, it would net twelve grand but cut, over twenty racks. Cameisha collected everyone's share and prepared to go make the buy but had to make a stop along the way.

****

"A-yo, remember to use your mirrors. Oh and hands at three and nine position like this," Jackie instructed and demonstrated as she drove them to the Department of Motor Vehicles.

"I know, I know, I got this," Meisha shot back confidently. She had aced the written part of the test, and Manny had given her lessons every day. She was ready.

When they arrived at the crowded building, they took a number and then a seat. Jackie whipped out her Kindle and began cracking up. She was laughing so much, so loud, that people stared over at her. Curiosity caused Cameisha to look over at the device.

"What you reading, yo?" Meisha asked, craning her neck to see.

"Yung Pimpin by Sa'id Salaam. This shit is crazy, yo!" Jackie answered and went back to reading and laughing.

Cameisha went inside her head and thought about her present future. A smile spread on her face as she decided to treat herself for passing her test. The thought had her so happy she danced in her seat.

"Number one thousand sixty four," a digital voice announced over the PA system.

Cameisha checked the number on her ticket against the voice and number flashing on the wall to confirm her turn.

"This me, yo!" She jumped up and tore off.

She was met outside by a plain Jane, forty-something license examiner. Jackie pulled up, got out, and handed over the key. Cameisha tried to butter the lady up with a smile, but she showed zero facial expression.

Meisha got in, buckled up, adjusted her mirrors, and followed direction.

"Left here, right here, merge into traffic," the woman ordered, jotting notes as they rode.

Cameisha nervously followed directions and tried to get a peek at the notes.

"Pull over there and parallel park between the cones," the examiner said, announcing the final task of the test.

Cameisha pulled over and executed a perfect three-point maneuver. The woman scribbled furiously then got out without a word. Meisha was on the verge of tears as she got out behind her.

"So, when can I take it again?" She pouted.

"No need, you passed," the woman replied with what may have been a smile.

"Yes, yes, yes!" Meisha cheered. She rushed around the car and hugged the woman so tightly she squeezed a real smile out of her. "Thank you, thank you, thank you!"

Cameisha broke off the awkward embrace and lauched into the Fat-Fat dance—the original. Jackie saw the commotion and came over to congratulate her friend. After doing her dance, she went back inside and took a cute picture for her driver's license.

With that out of the way, it was time to see Juan. Ironically, Juan wasn't the only one getting a drug-related visit.

****

Bilal was happily humming along with Sade as he tidied up his condo. He shot a glance at the velvet box on the coffee table and smiled. Inside of it was a one carat solitaire that he planned to give Cameisha along with his last name. A pounding on his front door rudely interrupted him. He snatched it open and was met by a badge.

"And how can I help you?" Bilal demanded to the man behind it.

"By being completely honest," Detective Walton quipped and barged in. The pudgy middle-aged black cop wore a look on his face as if something stunk. He was a piece of shit and probably smelled himself. "I see crime pays."

"Crime? I'm a doctor! You obviously have the wrong unit. Check your warrant again," Bilal huffed indignantly.

"No warrant. This is a social call," the cop said and plopped down on the sofa like he was invited. He tossed a manila folder on the coffee table knocking a picture of Cameisha down.

Bilal decided to ignore the slight in favor of seeing what was in the file. The cop was too smug, and it worried him. He flipped through the file with a frown that got deeper with every page.

"Good shit, huh?" Walton laughed.

"But I, I don't understand?" the doctor stuttered.

"What's to understand? You got greedy and got caught."

"I have nothing to do with this!" Bilal proclaimed and tossed the file back on the table.

The detective quickly picked it up and went through it.

"Okay, let's see. This is your pharmaceutical account, your IPO address, your approval codes. You approved a pill mill that doesn't exist. No physical address, just a P.O. Box. Really, really sloppy," he chided.

While those things pointed squarely at Bilal, it didn't mean much in itself. If he could get a confession out of the nervous man, he would have a case. After letting him absorb the facts, he pressed on.

"Help yourself while you can. Who are you selling the pills to? Are you working for someone? Ever been fucked in your ass? A pretty guy like you is gonna be a hit in prison," Walton teased.

"I can prove I have nothing to do with this," Bilal said, clinching his butt cheeks real tight. The thought of being violated propelled him into the room to retrieve his laptop. The cop wasn't sure what the sudden departure was about and put his gun under his thigh just in case.

"Here is my account!" Bilal said as he pounded in the password.

His jaw dropped when he saw that the orders did indeed come from his computer. All late at night, at times he never did business. All on dates he had dates with Cameisha.

"I . . . I . . . um, I think I know who did this?" he croaked.

****

"Watch this." Cameisha giggled to Jackie as she rang the doorbell to Juan's condo. High heels could be heard click-clacking on the marble just before the door was pulled open.

Angela sucked her teeth loudly at the sight of Cameisha. Tossing her head, she spun and stormed off. Both girls admired the diva's clothes, hair, and shoes as she marched away.

"That's a bad bitch," Jackie said honestly.

"So am I, just wait 'til I get my paper straight," Meisha promised. "And I'ma get my own."

Having been here enough to know where Juan would be, Cameisha led the way to the den. Inside, they found Juan and Manny making small talk.

"Hola, papi," Meisha sang, announcing her presence as she entered the room.

"Hola!" Juan cheered. He stood and opened his mouth wide to show off.

"Ooh, they took the wires out!" she cheered and rushed over.

Angela did a drive-by teeth suck as Cameisha touched his face.

"It's still a little sore, but I am ready to handle that business," Juan vowed with a glint of murder in his eye.

"We ready too," Meisha said, smiling at Jackie.

"Sure am," Jackie cosigned.

Cameisha passed off fourteen thousand dollars to Manny. It was for the purchase of nine ounces of coke and twenty ounces of weed. He passed a tote bag containing the work, and the deal was done.

"Sup with my 10k? I need as many of them as I can get," Juan asked.

"I'ma order it when I get back. Me and my girls taking a quick road trip tomorrow," Cameisha replied.

"Oh?" Jackie asked, hearing the plan for the first time herself.

"Yup, trust me. Y'all gone love it!"

Chapter 30

"You sure?" Cameisha pleaded as Dasia begged off the trip. "You can afford to miss a day. Besides, what's the point of getting money if we can't get the shit we want?"

"I'm cool, yo, plus my period just came on. I ain't tryna be stuck in no car bleeding. I'll just hold down the fort," Dasia shot back convincingly.

"True hustla for real!" Jackie laughed and gave her a pound.

The tension between old and new friend had dissipated once they started getting money together. Only fake niggas fall out over money. It brings real ones together.

"A'ight yo, I'ma brang you one back then," Meisha said mixing accents.

"Brang!!" Aqua laughed at her country grammar.

"And where we going anyway?" Jackie demanded again for the umpteenth time.

"And why?" Aqua added.

"The where is Mississippi, and the why is a surprise. Trust me, y'all gone love it!" Cameisha cheered and led the way out of the apartment.

The crew minus Dasia loaded into the Acura and set off. They hadn't even reached the expressway before Dasia snorted her first line. By the time the girls merged on I-20 West, she had inhaled large lines up each nostril. She was buzzing when she picked up her cell phone and made a call.

"Hey, baby," Lisa purred when she answered.

"Sup, ma. You stop by the grocery store for whip cream on your way over here," Dasia ordered.

"And just what is the whip cream for?" Lisa asked coyly.

"So I can suck it out your—I mean *my*—pussy!"

****

152

"Aww push it!" the girls screeched as they rapped along to a vintage Salt and Pepa song playing on the radio. They rapped, sang, and laughed all the way through Alabama and into Mississippi.

When a sign reading 'Longs, Mississippi' sped by overhead, Cameisha suddenly became sullen. The car grew eerily quiet from the mood change. It wasn't until she pulled off the highway and hit the main road did Meisha speak up.

"I have a confession for y'all." She sighed.

"It's cool, yo, whatever it is," Jackie assured her from the passenger's seat. She took her free hand in hers and gave it a comforting squeeze.

"We fam, yo," Aqua added from the back seat.

"Okay . . . um, well . . . the Fat-Fat dance, it's from a hamburger. A Fat-Fat burger. It's got meat, cheese, onions, bell peppers, and . . ."

"Wait!" Jackie frowned, throwing her hand away. "You mean to tell me you got the whole country dancing about a damn hamburger?"

"Not just any hamburger, a Fat-Fat burger," she whined.

"Ooh, I want one," Aqua declared.

"We 'bout to get one. That's why we here. I'm finally about to eat me a Fat-Fat burger," Cameisha said triumphantly.

Aqua clapped and did the dance as they drove towards the center of town.

"Huh?" Cameisha frowned when she drove past where the Fat-Fat Shack should have been.

There were plenty of new stores since she left but nothing where the restaurant should have been. She drove up to the supermarket that once provided the free samples she ate for dinner and turned around. She drove to the empty lot and pulled in. It was obvious from the charred remains that what was once here had burned to the ground.

Meisha got out and cried as she walked around the burned debris. A county worker taking pictures of the lot saw her and came over to check on her.

"Are you okay?" he asked tenderly at the young woman's tears.

"What happened? Where's the Fat-Fat Shack?" She sniffled.

"Great fiyah! Whole place went up like a matchbox. You could see the flame clear down to the creek," he replied. "Just last week."

"No!!!" Cameisha wailed, dropping to her knees. "I waited my whole life for one; now its over. It's over! My life is over." It was so sad, so *Color Purple*.

"Here, here, lil lady," the man said, pulling her up and into his embrace. He rocked gently as she sobbed and slobbered on his chest. "Why don't you just go 'round to the house and get cha one?"

"Huh?" Meisha said, suddenly pushing away so hard she almost knocked him down.

"Just go 'round to Ms. Anne's house. She fixes them up over there."

"Where?" she demanded, snatching him by the collar.

He barely got the address out before Cameisha was back in her car. The tires spun, sending gravel flying as she peeled out. She knew the area well, so she didn't need directions, especially since Ms. Anne lived a few blocks past where she grew up. When she neared their childhood home, Cameisha turned her head so she wouldn't have to look. Look or not look, she still felt it as she drove by. The history of abuse and neglect would not, could not, be ignored.

A steady stream of people and that delicious Fat-Fat smell said they were in the right place. People walked out with paper bags soaked in grease and smiling faces. One large lady couldn't wait and tore into the bag on the front lawn. She ripped away the wrapper and chomped into one. It exploded, sending a rivet of grease and special sauce running down her arm.

"Meisha!" Jackie screamed after Cameisha when she jumped from the still-moving car. She reached over and pushed the brake to stop the car then put it in gear.

Aqua bolted from the car and ran behind her.

"Give me ten Fat-Fat burgers!" Cameisha demanded, holding up a fistful of dollars to prove it.

"I want ten too!" Aqua announced, running in after her.

Ms. Anne just smiled her new smile, courtesy of a new pair of dentures, and got to work. She moved gracefully around the dirty kitchen, compiling the ingredients. First, she patted a ball of ground beef mixed with spices. Then slammed it on a cutting board and slapped it into a pattie.

"Um, I'm cool," Jackie said, frowning at the counter full of room temperature meat with all the roaches milling about. She knew one of them had to make it into one of those patties.

Ms. Anne dropped the patty into a black skillet of bubbling lard. After it went bacon, links, and pork patty. While the meat deep fried, she laid out a piece of wax paper. She placed an open bun on it and lathered it with lard from a small paintbrush that looked like it had been used to paint before. On went the patty, cheese, pork, cheese, onion, pepper, pork, bacon, cheese, and finally, lettuce, tomato, and special sauce. Ms. Anne topped it with the crown of the bun and proudly presented it to Cameisha.

"Hey, Fat-Fat," Meisha smiled gently at the burger. She gave it an affectionate kiss then opened wide. The burger squirted as she bit into it. "Arg!" Cameisha frowned at the disgusting taste.

Ms. Anne gave her a hurt look at the reaction. Not wanting to hurt the old lady, she forced herself to chew it and swallow it down.

"I think I'll save the rest for later," Meisha said, wrapping it up in the wax paper.

"Give me another one!" Aqua demanded as she polished off the first one.

Cameisha paid for the twenty burgers and headed out to the car. Jackie was right behind her, followed by Aqua going in on her third Fat-Fat burger.

This time when she neared her childhood home, she stared it down. Deciding it was time to face those demons, she whipped into the driveway and got out.

"I'll be right back," she explained to Jackie who asked a question with her facial expression.

The house was still as vacant as the day it was abandoned, but Meisha didn't venture inside. Instead, she went around to the back and stared into her old bedroom window. Ole man Grimes's smiling face appeared in her mind and then Maurice and all the other men who touched her.

"Good fo' you ass," she growled at the memory of the motel clerk's head exploding when she shot him. Then she thought of Maurice sitting on death row for killing Big Bessie and laughed. "Good fo' yo' ass too."

The good laugh was chased away by a good cry. The tears came and washed the smile from her face as Kathy's face clouded her vision. She, of course, had no way of knowing that the woman was buried in a cardboard box in Texas.

"Fucking junky!" Cameisha spat then spat as if the word had a bitter taste.

"You a junky too," a voice said so vividly she snapped her head from side to side. There was no one present, but the voice was definitely that of her mother.

"No, I ain't!" she yelled, stomping her feet like a frustrated five-year-old.

"I cain't tell. You poppin' them pills err day," Kathy teased. "Chile, you just like me."

"I'ma show you," Meisha vowed as she dug into her purse. She removed the pill bottle and scrambed to get the top off.

Once she had the bottle opened, she triumphantly slung the pills across the backyard.

"See, I'm just like my daddy!"

Chapter 31

"What's wrong with you?" Cameisha asked across the table for a third time over dinner.

"Hmm?" Bilal asked when her voice pulled him away from his thoughts. "Nothing," he replied, assuming correctly that she had asked the same question again.

His mind immediately went back to his dilemma. He saw all his hard work and sacrifice up in smoke behind a drug charge. Or—the alternative—snitching on the woman he loved. He cast a glance at her eyes and saw none of the telltale signs of drug use. Maybe it was all some mistake? Maybe he should get a lawyer or run away with her?

"You just need some pussy," Meisha decided. She had been neglecting him as of late because of all that was going on in the drug trade. If it hadn't been for Juan's ten thousand pull order, she wouldn't have found time now. "Some sex would be nice," her body said, tingling from the thought. "Check please."

The ride from the restaurant to Bilal's condo was quiet except for the radio. The sex was mechanical and detached, but since their bodies were in sync with each other, he came seconds after she did. Instead of the grateful kisses they usually shared after an orgasm, Bilal rolled off and closed his eyes. The only thing that could put a man to sleep quicker than a Thanksgiving dinner is a good nut. A minute later, Bilal was snoring— 'snoring' but not sleep.

Cameisha waited a few minutes, like always, before easing from the bed. She stared down at him for a minute before tip-toeing over to the computer. Bilal cracked his eyelids and watched her log onto his computer. He hoped she was going to post, like, or tag, but instead, she pulled up his pharmacy program.

Meisha placed the order and paid for it using a pre-paid credit card. She frowned at how long the order took to process. The anomaly unnerved her, and she was about to cancel the order. The approval code popped up a second before she aborted the mission. Delivery was set for three days. She got back in the bed and looked at Bilal sound asleep. She wiped a lone tear from his face and kissed his cheek before going to sleep herself. She needed some rest because tomorrow was a big day. Qisas.

****

"'Bout time you hung out with a nigga," Pedro said arrogantly then vowed, "I'ma fuck the dog shit out yo' black ass."

"That's so romantic," Jackie said dryly. She fought the urge to shoot him in his head for touching her thigh as he drove. "Yo, my girl, Meisha, told me you know how to throw that dick. Fuck that movie, let's go fuck."

"You ain't said shit!" he proclaimed and swung a wreckless u-turn in the middle of the street.

His dick had been hard since she called him and asked to link up. He had a date with Cynthia but wasn't going to make it. He wasn't going to make any more dates after tonight.

Pedro pulled into his raggedy apartment complex and sped towards his apartment. He skidded to a stop in an empty spot and jumped from the vehicle. He practically drug Jackie to the door in hopes of getting inside of her. They raced through the darkened apartment to the bedroom, hit the light, and . . .

"Surprise!!" Cameisha, Juan, and Manny cheered as they stepped inside.

The greeting was so cheerful Pedro actually smiled, until his mind processed the guns in their hands.

"What y'all doing here?" He frowned curiously.

"Ooh ooh! I won! You owe me a pound of weed," Meisha teased Juan. She had bet him that Pedro would ask a dumb ass question and won.

"I got you, mamacita." He laughed. His face turned to stone as he turned back to his victim. "Qisas, eye for an eye."

Pedro was about to talk some gansta shit, but Juan shot him in his face. The bullet tore through his jaw and into the wall. He turned to flee, but Meisha shot him in his knee. The thug rolled around on the floor, moaning and pleading for his life.

"Come, come now. Stop the whining. Did I whine when you shot me?" Juan asked, kneeling beside him.

Manny handed him some rope from a bag, and he began tying his arms and feet. Next, a super sharp machete came out of the bag.

"This is how we deal with snitches and thieves in my country," Juan growled as he straddled his back. "You ladies should leave now."

"Holla!" Jackie blurted and bolted. She was a killer and didn't mind killing, but she could tell something gruesome was on the horizon.

"I'm staying," Cameisha announced and drew closer.

Pedro looked directly into Cameisha's eyes when Juan pulled his head back and brought the knife around. A blood-curdling scream emitted from Pedro as his throat was cut. Meisha winced as he gurgled in his own blood. Juan moved the knife back and forth until the head came off cleanly.

"Aki," Manny said, holding open a plastic bag.

Cameisha took a second to have a word with the shocked expression he would take to hell with him. "See! This is what you get for being a grimy ass nigga," she chided.

"Manny, cut this piece of shit up and put him in the garbage where he belongs," Juan said after tossing the head in the bag. He turned to his adopted sister and asked, "Hungry?"

"Very! Let's get some scrimps," she cheered.

"I know a good Columbian spot."

Chapter 32

"Let me get a gram!" Cynthia demanded as she barged into Jackie and Cameisha's dorm room.

"A-yo, why don't you drag yo' damn bed down here as much as yo' ass be in here?" Jackie spat.

"What do you mean?" the airhead asked sincerely.

"Chile, you know you gotta get that from Dasia and dem at the 'partment," Cameisha advised.

Just like with the weed, Jackie only handled larger amounts of blow. If you needed an eight ball to an ounce, this was the spot. Anything under, go holla at Dasia. Dasia offered to handle the blow while Aqua handled the weed. The system seemed to be working because every penny was accounted for. That was Meisha's job—counting cash.

"The stuff y'all got is better than what they got over there," the druggie pouted.

"It's the same shit!" Jackie shot back. She still felt some kinda way about the connection between Cynthia and Pedro. If it was up to her, she would have killed her, too, and been done with it.

Cameisha was convinced she was duped and spared her. She was going to regret that decision one day, but that's part three.

"Nuh uh! This stuff barely gives me a buzz," Cynthia said, holding up half a gram from out of her purse.

"Where you get this from?" Meisha demanded even though she recognized the crew's distinctive pink baggies. The coke inside, however, was not theirs. This was cut to shit.

"From y'all. It don't even do nothing," she whined sadly.

"Must be the wrong batch. Yo, Jackie, give her one of those eights. My bad," Meisha directed, keeping the sample.

"Thank you," Cynthia cheered gratefully.

As soon as she cleared the room, Meisha grabbed her phone.

"Sup, Meisha?" Aqua sang upon answering the line.

"Chillin' yo. Yo, Cynthia been by there?"

"Last night. She came to holla at Dasia though."

"Let me holla at D," Meisha asked.

"She went out with that chick, Lisa, last night. She ain't back yet," Aqua replied.

Cameisha frowned at the girl's name. The one time she met Lisa, she kept looking Meisha up and down like a man looks at a woman, or like a woman who likes pussy like men like pussy, and men like pussy a lot.

"She leave anything?"

"Yeah, I'm holding it down," Aqua said proudly.

"A'ight yo, I'ma fall through," Meisha said and hung up.

"Sup yo?" Jackie frowned, sensing something amiss.

"'Bout to find out."

Cameisha rushed over to the apartment and collected one of the gram packages Dasia left beind. She could tell off the muscle that it was the same cut up crap Cynthia had. She went into the secret stash and took out a gram of pure coke and set off to see an expert.

****

"Hey, Cameisha. What brings you by?" Samantha sang when she answered the knock and saw Cameisha.

"Sup yo," Meisha replied stoically and barged in. She looked around the cluttered space that resembled a lab more than a dorm room. "Need a favor, yo. I got an ounce of loud if you do it."

"Sure!" Samantha cheered as if free weed were a touchdown.

"I need you to test these for me," she said, handing her the samples. One was the gram from Dasia, the other from Jackie's bomb, and finally, the pure coke from the stash. "I'll be back in an hour."

"I'll be done by then," Samantha called after her as she fled the room.

Cameisha went back to the dorm to grab an ounce to pay for the test. Jackie tagged along when she went back for the results.

"Hey, guys! Come in. I have something amaaazing to show you!" the hyper scientist announced, pulling her guests inside.

"Okay this," Samantha began, holding up the coke from Jackie, "is roughly sixty percent pure cocaine. It's cut with . . ."

"I know, I know," Cameisha cut in, cutting her off since she knew what it was cut with.

"Okay, and this is the same cocaine cut with . . . the same stuff only its twenty-five percent pure."

Cameisha could only shake her head. Math was one of her best subjects, and two and two added up to Dasia stealing from the crew. Why and how was the question because all the money added up.

"What?" Jackie asked to the questions twisting Meisha's face.

"Tell you as soon as I figure it out myself," Cameisha shot back. "What about the last one?"

"Glad you asked. Let me show you something amazing," Samantha said in awe as if she had discovered a new species. In a way, she had.

"This is four grams of ninety-eight percent pure cocaine. I made if from the gram you gave me," she said, beaming with pride.

"Wait a second . . . you took one gram and made four? Same strength? How is that possible?" Cameisha asked in elation mixed with fear.

"Quite simple actually. Well, not really simple because I used a process I developed to activate inert substances, forcing them to take on the qualities of a particular host. You have to use a magtrometer and . . ."

"You know what this means, Jackie?" Cameisha asked as Samantha rambled on about the process.

"Yeah, yo, you 'bout to be the queen of cocaine out this bitch!" Jackie exclaimed.

"Nah yo. Fuck the queen. I'ma be the king, just like Daddy!"

Epilogue

"Is that her?" Detective Walton demanded as Cameisha pulled into the parking lot of the P.O. Box to pick up her 10k pill order.

Bilal only sighed as her presence killed all the excuses he made for her. He wanted to save her, but even though he shook his head no his mouth said, "Yeah, that's her."

"Heads up, people. Subject has arrived in a white Acura. Nobody move until she has taken receipt of the package."

Cameisha was bopping her head to the latest jam by Domie Daddy as she pulled in. Being sober the last few days had her happier than being high. With this new clarity, she could see her friend had a drug problem. She needed an intervention, not a killing, which is what theft usually called for. Besides, with her own recent problems, she couldn't be a hypocrite.

The moment Meisha cut the engine, she went to high alert. Before she opened the door, she scanned the area. Her brain processed danger as she stepped out. Something was off. It was too still for so many people to be out and about. As she looked around, she counted at least four different sets of eyes looking back at her. None smiled or waved, just quickly averted their eyes when she made contact.

Something wasn't right, but the large payday urged her on. As she crossed the parking lot, her father's voice rang in her head.

"If you feel like something ain't right, it ain't . . ."

Dope Girl 3 Coming Soon

163